ALSO BY LLOYD HOLLIS CROOKS

Ice and Eyes in the Sun: True Love Comes Late, Sometimes.

Grenada Ghost

Peeping Through the Keyhole

A Novel
By Lloyd Hollis Crooks

Patricia Belcon, Ph.D.
Editor

Published by
Wayne Brathwaite Publishing
519 East 26th Street
Brooklyn, New York 11210
E-mail: crooksgg519@aol.com
Ph: 1-718-693-7610 / 1-646-265-3239
www.lloydholliscrooks.com

Library of Congress Control No. 2015908332

ISBN 0-9666296-4-7

Printed in the United States

Book designer: nkkoprinting@gmail.com

This book is dedicated to

All the Immigrants—
Those who came to this country and suffered hardships
and are still suffering hardships;
Those who have climbed above their hardships, and are
reaping the largesse of this great country; and
Those with "derailed dreams" who are still struggling,
and are still searching to see the light at the end of the tunnel to
become American citizens.

Reviews

Peeping Through the Keyhole is not only a sexual text. It is, for sure, about the sociology I know in the 1950's. I have worked in the Trinidad Oilfields, West Indies, for 40 years; and I have witnessed, first hand, the prejudice of the British colonial expatriates in Trinidad and Tobago. I confirm what Stude Bakka says about those expatriates during his childhood. Zelda Hedgpine is my hero. As a sociology glutton, I didn't want **Peeping** to end.

Edward Noble

I could never have foreseen the ending in **Peeping Through the Keyhole.** In this novel, one sees the tomfoolery of lovers. Nonetheless, it is a serious, thoughtful novel about sociological matters. It is easy to read. I enjoyed it.

Atiba Taariq

Zelda and Hector Hedgpine are both sick in and out of love. Stude Bakka and his sociologist friend, Dr. Eli Balboza, had me cracking up with their *Ebonics*. **Peeping Through the Keyhole** shows how sex can destroy us. This novel is a page turner.

A'dhayna Nehisi

Acknowledgments

Thank you, Dr. Patricia Belcon, for taking time off from your busy lecturing schedules at Medgar Evers College to edit my book, and for giving me your lucid critique. You always impart your intellectual generosity in class and out of it, and I thank you for that, too.

Thank you, Anita Scanterbury, for proofreading my text so diligently at such short notice.

Thank you, Austin H. Tuitt, Community Organizer, poet, musician, and lecturer, for giving me permission to use a verse from *Pearls of Inspiration* dedicated to "Oneness."

Thank you, Georgia Rosemarie Haye, for giving me the idea for this book.

All my thanks go to you—you know who you are—for telling me your searing and sad story of the domestic abuse that you suffered for so many years, on which my story is based.

Peeping
Through the Keyhole

a Novel

LLOYD HOLLIS CROOKS
"True Love Can Be a Burden,"
says the Facebook Lover

1

Fate has no favorites. It is an occurrence in life that comes without warning to praise us, to uplift us, to blame us, or to hurt us. Cinderella loses her slipper but her fate is not a dreadful mishap, but a joyful occasion to uplift her when the prince finds her slipper and marries her. On the other hand, Zelda Hedgpine lost the comfort and happiness she enjoyed with the Dictator and her parents in her lovely home in Caracas, Venezuela.

She lost that precious comfort of her homeland when she came to New York in search of a place where she can practice her hidden desires for romance with many men. But, unlike Cinderella, Zelda's fate was unfortunate because she makes her love a moving target for the man who loves her dearly. She wants another man who loves her, but that man is an honorable man, and he stifles his love for her because he is her husband's best friend.

The private conversations between Zelda Hedgpine, the daughter of wealthy Venezuelan parents, and me stayed permanently on my mind as the flesh on my black body. Zelda tells me about the sadistic, domestic, and racial violence she suffered not only under her first husband, David Ide, when she came to New York, penniless and homeless, only knowing a spattering of the English language. She was dependent on a Good Samaritan's graces for food and shelter. And with tears streaming from her brown eyes, she was cathartic; and she trusted to divulge secrets about her and her mother's sex life, and why she used sex as her tool to bargain for survival. She preferred to sell her body, underpriced, than to beg for money or food to appease her hunger. She said beggars have no pride or self-worth. The only advice I had for her on our first day of friendship was what E.B. White, the co-author of *Elements of Style*, writes, "No one should come to New York unless he [or she] is willing to be lucky."

My knowledge of Spanish is nil, but with the help of my hand gestures and inflections of my body movements, I knew Zelda understood White's words of advice to immigrants when she looked into my eyes and bowed affirmatively. Zelda's thirst for my friendship was seen in her eyes as her knowledge of English improved, and I wanted her friendship too, so I spoke nonstop of my wayward boyhood to get her undivided attention. I had learned from my atheist friend, John Jules, that in speaking of one's childhood you will always find a seed to plant and grow friendship.

In my youth, I was thankful to the prostitute who became my friend. She showed me the way when I was lost at the crosswords of not knowing what I should know about sex as my body craved for her. I was seventeen, and she advised me of the tantric method of delaying climax. Her advice became an asset in my early life at a time when there was no Viagra or Cialis on the chemist's shelf. Talking to Zelda was comfortable for me, and to make her feel at home in my company I continued to speak of my boyhood with the hope that she will talk of her girlhood.

It was as if I was a boy again at the Oropouche seashore in Trinidad, West Indies, where I watched the fishermen throwing out their nets to catch the tasty fry-me-dry herrings. However, and at the same time, my inquisitive mind was comparing the fishermen's skill with their nets with the prostitutes' art of fishing for men, with their invisible nets—their suave sexuality, their survival instincts, and their guile.

The ways of prostitutes always perked my interest. This was because of my mother's "sociology of need" when she stirred her pot of gruel and prayed for better days to come. She will look as if she knew what I was thinking and say, "Stude, a prostitute who needs food for herself will wait for customers. But a prostitute who needs food for her children will look for customers until she finds them."

My mother's sociology of need gave me the knowledge of why some women become short-term prostitutes. As a result, I vowed never to look down on prostitutes as women of disrepute, but as drowning women, who will hold on to a straw for the survival of their family.

As Zelda's English gradually improved, to make her continue to trust me, I told her why girls had told me their fools'-paradise dreams: Dreams that were hidden in their bosoms and squeezed their puny-coat-hook breasts. Those girls trusted me because I only told the stones in my mother's backyard that was crowded with thorns and rosebush of their joyous kissing romance in their convent-school uniforms when they sat in the back of the Trinidad Government Railroad bus. And I had told the girls' most sacred secrets of when they lost their virginity to bigger boys only to the hogs that my brother, Seth, fed in the backyard. The hungry swine never cared to listen to my tell tales because their primordial interest was snapping at each other's ears to get the most fodder emptied into their troughs.

As an adult, women who brought me into their clan knew, instinctively, that I will listen to their stories, shameful or not, without condemning them. My mother's stories were not make-believe; they were similar to other women's stories of hunger, of pain, of faith and fate, and of the insincerity of the men in their lives. They held on to these men because society with its unfair rules for women made it difficult for women to survive without men.

When I became Zelda's friend and confidant, she never stopped telling me why her tears will boomerang on her domestic-violence lovers whose initial showing of pretentious love to her had the depth of their 'bad breaths.' She questioned my friend, Hilda, who had told me, "If I had to do it again, I will try 'sexless companionate friendship' with a man and wait and see if it will work before I commit my body to him." Yet Hilda fell in love quickly and fell out of love just as quickly regardless of the fact that she had warned herself, 'to never let her craving for sex allow her garden be erotically scented and watered by a man because he is handsome and has a silver tongue.'

Zelda loves literature, and she loves a man with a silver tongue. She's alike Hilda. That *verba solemnia* (solemn vow), to think with her head and not with her vagina goes on the back burner when 'nature calls.'

I came to the unscientific, and probably unfair, conclusion that Zelda was already a nymphomaniac when I met her. She said,"I prefer to be a 'jump-off gal,' not having a steady partner because I am afraid of commitment. I do not understand American men because they never keep their promises. But I will never be left without a chair when the music of love stops no matter how great the competition."

I am a man who loves women's company. I study their varied personas. I've learned our hubris telegraphs our downfall with cadences, sometimes the same as Babylon's. Our downfall wagons with it disappointments in our treasure hunting, in our climbing the ladder of success, and life presents new issues. At times, they are unclear as opaque ore; and we could never have seen in advance the misfortune ahead of us.

Death is the only inevitable fate. "Sit back and enjoy life today which is a certainty rather than waiting on the next coming of your Lord Jesus Christ."

Whenever, in jest, I had provoked my deceased wife, a pastor by avocation, to enjoy life while she's alive, rather than waiting on the next coming of Christ, she called me "the Devil incarnate." I will never print the blue adjectives she had called me that made me laugh aloud.

I told Zelda, "Humor should be the glue in romance." I also told her, "I'm loath to enter once more into matrimony because I still think of when I was jilted by my first love. She fell deeper in love with an Anglican minister. The cleric, I imagined, was romantic in and out of bed, like King Solomon and his wife, Tirzah. My love for any woman moves with my mood, and I don't intend to change my way, especially as I've not remarried.

Zelda's stare burned my eyes when I said my love moves with my mood. I saw her beautiful teeth; some spliced with white gold. She wanted to hear more of the happenings in my youth, and I told her more because I had an ax to grind. That ax was keeping Zelda next to me, to admire the deep curves of her healthy body, and to inhale the scent from her.

"Tell me something of your growing up, Stude," she said.

I grew up in the forties in Fyzabad, a little oil

town in colonial Trinidad and Tobago, which was then ruled by Great Britain and its laws. At that time every school child must stand in the broiling-hot sun or in the rain, waved the Union Jack, and sing: "Rule Britannia, Britannia Rules the Waves," in celebration of British traditions and King George V's Birthday.

Seth refused to learn those school songs and was punished by his teacher, but his mettle and sense of individualism from such an early age against British colonialism made him my hero.

I, on the other hand, waved the Union Jack, sang the praises of Great Britain aloud and with a happy look on my face and joy in my heart. I let my teacher see me and hear me because I did not want to be punished. Unlike Seth, I played the game with my teachers and my lovers as early as the date of when my urine became yellow.

Zelda asked, "Who is-Seth?" I told her, and then I morphed into my knowledge of women who suffered from domestic abuse and how those abusers should be punished. She listened with rapt attention, and I spoke nonstop.

Seth was two years my senior, and we were inseparable. We even accompanied each other to the latrine which is a primitive toilet in the backyard. We lived with our one-parent mother in a cedar-board barracks that rested firmly on rough-board flooring, which was the foundation for the barracks. The roof was covered with rusty galvanized iron and leaked when it rained. And when the rain really poured, a tributary ran from one apartment to the other.

Each tenant had two rooms, about twelve yards by fifteen yards. The partitions that separated each tenant from the others were thin as dried immortelle leaves, trampled by cows' hooves. If a humming bird, our national bird, loses its way in flight, and drops through a hole in the zinc roof, it can put its tiny beak on any partition and bore its way through and exit freely to freedom.

I could sense Zelda comparing in her mind her life of luxury as a child compared to mine and Seth's. I drew my chair closer to her. We were now pals eating a frugal meal at McDonalds. I continued to relate nuggets of my life as a youth in Fyzabad. Our expired occupation of the table with our empty paper plates annoyed the hungry customers, who had no seats. I began to call her Zee and she smiled approvingly. She nodded for me to continue talking.

In those barracks I learned social transformation in its original manifestations in words and deeds.

I also learned the habits of oilfield men without a "humility muscle" and without humanity who flourished in those Fyzabad barracks. Those observations were evident: The colonial ruler enacted no domestic laws to protect women from men's harm; and if they did, none was exercised to punish those beasts with two legs.

Those beasts were muscular oilfield men who beat their wives and common law wives as often as they breathe. I was eight when I told a policeman, "Go quick! Go quick, and lock up Mr. Cheeseman! He is beating up Miss Cheeseman with a bull pestle." He replied, "Little boy, that is not your business! That is husband and wife's business. Run to school, quick, before I lock you up!"

I knew my mother's law: If she had a husband or a no-good man who hit her, she would have cooked him with boiling water, mixed with hot oil while he slept on his corn-straw mattress, snoring, and dreaming of hurting his mate in the morning. But that never happened. Thank God. To me, my mother was the lone and bravest woman in those barracks.

My mother didn't depend on any man for money because she worked for everything she needed for herself and her two boys. She ploughed the barren fields as if she were a Caterpillar tractor; and she planted seeds that yielded crops that she sold in Fyzabad market to get money. She also washed and ironed white people's clothes. And, because of the way she toiled to earn a living, her determination to kill the man who hit her would have been conveyed, without words of contrition, to a jury of the colonial master's choice.

"No man could hit me," was her mantra; and she looked at Seth and me when she swore vengeance to "any stinking bitch." That's the way she described men, and she crossed her index fingers and put them on her lips with the sign of the crucifix. Mammy did that to warn Seth and me that when we become men, and if we hit our wives, our fate should be death or disfigurement by the women we hurt. When I said that, Zelda's eye popped and she begged me to continue speaking.

There was another woman somewhat like my mother, but with a different way of making a living. Her penchant for getting men's respect after they amused themselves on her bed became a warning to other men. She was called Evena L, because there was another Evena, whose comportment was so taciturn that she hardly spoke. Fyzabad's men became aware of Evena L's motto.

It was rumored that butcher-man Boysie who did not pay her the full price for sex lost his nature. And not even drinking a mixture of a boiled-root potion, a concoction by Papa Neezah, the famous shaman herbalist and voodoo priest, could cure Boysie's erectile dysfunction. Boysie could no longer, with pride, boast to his friends of his hard erection that made women scream in pain when he mounted on them.

As a little kid, I taxed my intelligence to know what "a rock-hard erection" meant when my mother gossiped with Evena L. My mother had sent me to Boysie to buy half pound of meat to cook in peas soup, and when I saw Boysie's blood-stained apron tied in front of him, my only reason adduced as to why he was wearing that soiled apron, was to hide his "lost rock-hard erection." I went home and told my mother, "Mammy, I saw Boysie; and he lost his rock-hard erection." She laughed endlessly, chased me out of the kitchen, and said, "Boy, plenty breeze is blowing. Go outside and fly your kite."

The words I knew best of barracks people were: "That is the woman that that man is living with; that is the man who does beat up the woman he is living

with; that man does beat up his wife every payday."
I did not know if those women in the barracks were
wives or common-law wives; all I knew was the man
and the woman lived in the same room, and the woman was called Miss Irene, Miss Dora, etc., because
children only knew the women's first names and had
to put "Miss" before their names to show respect to all
women, married or unmarried.

However, I could hear the blows that were
rendered by burly men, and I could hear the women
eating those blows in silence for the other barracks
dwellers not to know of the domestic violence they
endured. But the partition hid nothing, and I knew
who gave Miss Irene the "black" eye and why Miss
Rosa had her head bandaged so early in the morning.

The abusive men worked in the oilfields owned
by the colonial magnates and their pay-day floggings
to their spouses were clockwork. I remember that because my mother would talk to Seth and me at dusk
while lighting her coal pot. In the coal pot were brown
paper and wood chips underneath the coal; pitch oil
would be thrown in the coal pot and then my mother
lit the coal with a match. Sometimes she had to get a
lit coal from a neighbor to light her fire because she
had no money to buy matches.

As the coal glowed, my mother said, "Am sure Harry is coming home drunk after he lost his money from gambling. The fool cannot read, and he cannot count and memorize the cards that passed. He is going to beat up Dora when she asks him for money to buy food for the children." So said, so done!

After a while, little me, like my mother, prophesied all the barracks-women-payday beatings like clockwork. Zelda looked down and looked away. She was in a world known to her from what was coming from my lips.

E. Wayne McDonald, the artistic director of the Caribbean Cultural Theatre at Medgar Evers College, describes Caribbean people's troubles and tales in "dub prose." *Tellin we own story*, is McDonald's favorite dub-prose phrase which is the ethnic twang that comes off the lips of Caribbean people without veneer, or syntax, but understood.

Ras Osagyefo, "the brilliant spoken-word artist in the dub poetry tradition," raps poetically in *Psalms of Osagyefo*. In his poem, *Hands That Rock the Cradle*, he writes: "Dem ah talk about the hands/ That rock the cradle/ Yet no mention is made about the/ Ones underneath the table." The hands underneath the table could have been the hands of the sadist men in Fyzabad barracks who beat their common law wives mercilessly, or the hands underneath the table could have been the hands of the man who put his boots on Zelda Hedgpine's sore body.

That beast in the likeness of a man was able to hurt Zelda because his finger prints that would have revealed his criminality ahead of time were hidden below the table. But, without holding on to Osagyefo's words of wisdom, I will tell my story of Zelda Hedgpine's fate in the America she loves. She wanted me to tell you because of her lack of English.

Hector and I saw Zelda the same day. But he saw her outline from a distance, not her face. I met her first. Zelda was a battered woman who poured out her guts and told me her life with her first husband, David Ide."He beat me like if he were beating a snake on hot sand that had no hole to slither into and hide."

Unlike when I was a boy and I lived in Fyzabad I now know, if a man abuses his wife or common law wife, his abuse is called "domestic violence." Nowadays his wife can call 911 or that special number to complain about her domestic-violence abuser. Today there are shelters for abused women to bide their time in safety. The law will punish or incarcerate husbands or boyfriends who violently abuse their wives or girlfriends—whether those domestic abusers are politicians, men of the law, or sportsmen with the label of MOST VALUABLE PLAYER. But is that really always the case in the United States that these laws punish men abusers guilty of physically hurting their spouses? At times, yes; other times, the women were killed by their abusive spouses when the laws applied by some judges were dumb laws.

Zelda is no longer an abused wife. She has become a part of the American culture that weighs heavily on the side of animals, children, and women. Now she is doing the messing up of men's minds.

Every day Zelda sends a love letter to a new lover by text or on *Facebook*. She breathes through social media—*Email, Instagram, Tweeting, Texting, Facebook, Access Hollywood, Entertainment Tonight, The Wendy Williams Show, TMZ,* and the names go on and on. When Zelda's English was improved, I had asked her, "If you were born before social media ruled your life, what would you have done?" Her glib answer was, "That's why I wasn't born then. I am of the millennial generation. I am not like you, Stude Bakka, of the silent generation, stuck in the past. I am a social-media woman in love, in life, and in sex, right up to the minute."

We laughed and drank black coffee. I said, "As old as I am, I know how to get into your social-media thong."

"Why not do it now, Stude Bakka? Only two of us are at home."

We giggled as children, who didn't want the teacher to hear us, and kicked each other with our toes underneath the table. As our giggling simmered, she was texting another letter, but she didn't let me see the addressee. Neither did I care to know the addressee. I hate texting with a passion but I, too, indulged in texting because she sends me sex texts for me to weigh her decision versus mine in certain matters of love before sending them to a new friend or lover.

I don't know why she uses me as a pitch fork to get me in trouble with her husband. But, I am glad at times that she lets me read her texts to other men, because reading them gives me the opportunity to know, of her sex life, her trickery, and her guile. Coming to think of it, another reason is, she is using me to get English 101, or she has an ax to grind.

Zelda and I had spent an evening listening to Miles Davis at the Village Vanguard in lower Manhattan. When we detrained in Brooklyn, I accompanied her to her door without saying goodbye, but I kept looking at her. She is a very attractive woman, and I admire attractive women.

When I see an attractive woman, my nerve cells wake me up to stare at her until she goes out of sight. When Hector tells me, "Look at that beautiful woman passing by," if she is not attractive, to me, I look at her and turn away.

I kept looking at Zelda's queenly carriage in boots fitted up to her knees. I also looked at the shape of her body and the texture of her dark-brown skin. She was casually dressed in a short top, and her mid-riff shone like quicksilver on glass in the midday sun. Her slacks, jersey material, stuck on her just right. Yet I could see the calm contortions of her derrière as each cheek moved teasingly to the beat of music in her ear.

"See you later, Stude."

"What time, Zee?"

"Wait on my text."

"Make sure the text is for me."

She laughed aloud, looked at me, and danced to the salsa beat in her ear. I knew it was salsa music because Antonio Carlos Jobim is her idol. She always listens to Brazilian music, and when she speaks to her Brazilian friends she mixes Spanish and Portuguese as if both romance languages are one and the same.

She told me on our way from an evening at the World Trade Tower plaza before it was bombed by terrorists when Hector was out of town on his Homeland Security assignment, "The only match to Jobim in my bed is Miles Davis' muted trumpet playing *I Fall in Love Too Easily.*"

At that time her English was at the level of a third grader, but her knowledge of all genres of music blew my mind. But my mind was burned when she told me she likes stream jazz because it incorporates classical and chamber music; and she is a fairly good pianist. In Caracas she had recitals in her house for the Dictator and his friends, who looked as hoodlums. Her knowledge of life's meanderings in good and evil is kept close to her vest, and I never pried to know of them. I did it once, and I regretted it.

In our discussions, I saw that Zelda was no lightweight in world affairs. She only gives bits of her background, if asked. But being in the company with my dear friend, Dr. Eli Balboza, whom I call Dr. El, because of my endearment for her, I learned a lot of what is expected of people. Dr. El taught me how to pick out a fool in daylight. I knew Zelda was no fool in daylight, neither was she when the moon was crescent shaped. Dr. El told me a fool is always eager to let people know how smart he or she is; and when you let the fool speak, the fool's lexicon has three words: "I know that."

Once, before Zelda and I became real buddies, I jokingly used the 'I-know-that' style on her. I tried to get her to impart personal information of her life in Caracas.

She replied, "Write me a love letter, and I will tell you everything."

"Okay. The mailman will take my letter to your address."

She shouted, "*Solamente una vez.*" Then swirled, her booty in first, as the elevator went up.

2

On my way home I couldn't stop thinking why Zelda said "*Solamente una vez.*" Doesn't that mean: You belong to my heart? Why my heart? I questioned myself.

I taxed my memory and remembered the first time I saw her up close was at a bodega on Nostrand Avenue. Hector remained outside so he didn't see her. She barely knew a word in English. I asked for a box of cornflakes, original, and she did not understand what I said. She ran to the back of the store, and a man came and told me, "She know no English."

Two years later, my craving was for Spanish food, and I went to a restaurant on Flatbush Avenue that a friend recommended. There were other customers whom she had served before and had given her big tips, but she showed no interest to serve them. She whispered to me, "I have to serve those roaches, but I hate them. They know I am looking for a place, but I'd rather sleep in DUMBO." DUMBO means Down

Under Manhattan Bridge Overpass. Her accent was heavy. I whispered just as softly, "I have a one-bedroom apartment to rent."

"Where?"

"Not far from here."

"When I bring the bill, write the address on it. And don't tip me."

"Why?"

"I'll tell you why if you rent me the apartment."

I was employed as a partner's secretary at the law firm of Sage Gray Todd and Sims, and I wanted to hang out after work because I had a hectic day transposing many depositions from shorthand to English. I had stopped my bad habit of going to look into peepholes in Manhattan. Instead, I got on the ferry boat to Staten Island and returned on the next departing boat to Bowling Green, New York. Suddenly, I remembered a woman is coming to see the empty apartment. But, somehow, I knew she'd wait even if I were five hours late.

I was four hours late. It was summer and Pizza Hut on my block is never closed. Just as I thought, she was sitting there, a pizza before her, untouched.

I came at her back and said, "You bought pizza because you wanted a place to sit and wait for me."

"Oh my god! I rang your bell so many times, and your neighbors were looking at me as a thief. If you will eat my pizza, I'll get them to hot it in their oven."

I sat and waited for the pizza to be reheated. "You did not tell me your name."

"And you did not write your name on the check. My name is Zelda Peña."

"I am Stude Bakka." The pizza was hot, and I stretched for it.

"No, Mr. Bakka. You are too well dressed to walk with a greasy bag."

I smiled, and I noticed she had a traveling bag. "I do not eat pizza. When I came to New York a slice of pizza cost a quarter."

She looked at my attire. "In this hot weather you keep on your jacket, Mr. Bakka?"

"My memory is kaput; and I'm afraid if I'd taken off my jacket I would have left it by one of the peep-holes in Manhattan."

"I like your sense of humor, Stude Baker."

"Call me Stude."

"I like calling you by both names."

"Have it your way." I opened the door to the apartment.

"I like it! I love it!" Then her excitement waned.

I knew why her excitement diminished. "If you can swear that you'll be a good tenant, and you will not call 411 when there's no heat, we can bargain on a price."

She looked at me. "True?"

"Zelda Peña, I'm a man of my word."

"In Caracas, my friends call me Zee, and I'd like you to call me Zee. My mother calls me Badzee, and I'm praying that one day I'd see her before she dies."

"Are you bad?"

"To my mother, I was really bad. We'll talk about my mother and my badness if I'm living upstairs."

"The apartment is yours."

She started to cry. I left her in the apartment, went downstairs, and put on my jeans and T-shirt. I went back upstairs and knocked on her door.

"Come in. My tears are dry. Please, let me hug you and thank you, Stude Bakka. You are my Angel, and if I never see another, that's okay."

She hugged me, and kissed me on my lips.

"Zee, it's getting late. You should leave and come back with your things tomorrow."

"It's Friday, and I'm sleeping here tonight. All my belongings are in that." She pointed at her bag, and her joy was sufficient to share with all the sad souls in the world.

The tenor of her voice put a lump in my throat. I went in my basement and brought up a twin mattress, bed frame, sheets, pillows, pillow cases, towels, wash cloths, soap, toilet paper, and a new robe. I told her she can use my kitchen in the meantime. She showered in her bathroom and sang *Solamente una vez*.

I remember that that song in English is *You Belong to My Heart/Now and Forever*. My mother sang that song when she was washing her clothes in a wooden tub with a corn husk. I often wondered then if that song was for my father, who left her with Seth and me and married another woman. Or, if that song were for my stepfather who had just moved in, and by her keen observations she felt he loved his stepchildren.

Zelda got up early Saturday morning, and her domestication made me think that she knew what men had for breakfast.

"Zee, who showed you where to find the things in my kitchen to make breakfast?"

"I work in a restaurant."

"Why you told me not to tip you when you

served me in the restaurant?"

"I didn't want those roaches to see."

"You shouldn't call people roaches."

"They didn't know I speak Spanish; and I didn't like the names they called me because they tipped me. They called me a *puta*; that means I'm a whore."

"They should know if you are working in a bodega, Spanish would be the language of the owner's choice."

"Whenever they spoke in Spanish I always brought the wrong meal. And whenever they called me *puta*, I laughed and say thank you, sir. They came to the conclusion that I only speak English. I call those kinds of people roaches. Do you like the way I cooked eggs with baccalao?"

"It's delicious. Isn't Saturday a busy day at the restaurant?"

"Yes, but I'm not going to work there again. From Monday, I'll be looking for a new job. This weekend I will be decorating my room. Stude Bakka, I do not know the words to thank you in English. When I get a better job, I will look for an English teacher, and I will put more money on my rent."

"I can help you with English, if you will trust me."

"Stude Bakka, I will trust you with my life."

"Please, please, don't! My mother told Seth and me that we should always cast our bread on the water."

"What does that mean?"

"When we give, someday someone will give us, and more." She passed the butter for the bread. "I don't eat butter. The eggs and baccalao hit my ribs, and I want to belch out the gas in my stomach."

"Is it that good?"

"Yes. Where would you go to look for a job? What kind of job you have in mind?"

"I want to work in a nice restaurant as a waiter. I like a job where I see lots of people. Where do you work, Stude Bakka?"

"In the Wall Street neighborhood."

"I've never been in that neighborhood."

"Hector will be here this weekend, and the three of us can go and look at the Wall Street bull, walk through Battery Park, go up the World Trade Towers, take a ride to Staten Island on the ferry, the works."

"Who is Hector?"

"My friend. He lives in a beautiful apartment in Park Slope with elevator service."

"Where is he now?"

"He works for Homeland Security."

"What he does?"

"He never tells me. And I never ask."

"I notice you are the same. You take me in without a recommendation, and you never inquired why I prefer to sleep in DUMBO than to be friendly with those Roaches."

"Down Under Manhattan Bridge Overpass is not safe for anyone to sleep. But, please, don't call people roaches."

"They called me a whore, and said how they will fuck me in my mouth and shit on my face. I took their tips because I had to put it in a pan to share with the other waiters. Otherwise, I would never even touch their money."

"Zee, I enjoyed breakfast. I will clean up. Please, leave my kitchen." That was my way of getting her off the Roaches.

"My great grandfather had a car that sounded just like your name. It was a Studebaker. The front and the back had the same shape."

"Is that so?"

"Would you allow me to prepare lunch for you and Hector when he comes tomorrow?"

"We will be eating out."

On Sunday Zee prepared breakfast for both of us again. Then she left and returned nicely dressed. I informed her Hector always comes promptly at 1.02 p.m. "If you hear three bells, it's he. Open the door if I am in the shower, and keep him company. He will understand if you mix Spanish with English. You don't have to hide from us as you did when you worked in the bodega on Nostrand Avenue."

"Oh my god! It was both of you. I noticed he remained way outside. I thought both of you were Immigration policemen."

The bell rang at 1.02 p.m., and she opened the door. "Come in, Hector. Mr. Bakka is in the bathroom."

Hector opened his mouth, and left it opened for a minute. "Thank you. Are you Stude's sister who lives in Trinidad?"

"My name is Zelda Peña, the new tenant. I don't have to tell you to take a seat because Stude has been rattling about you since I came."

"When?"

"Last night."

"Who are you?"

"His new tenant who lives upstairs."

I shouted. "What's the time? Hector is expected 1.02."

"It's 1.04 and he is here," Zelda said.

"Hector, I'm dressing in the bathroom. Help yourself."

"With the new tenant?" Hector asked.

"That, too," I shouted louder.

Zelda smiled. "Hector, I see both of you love humor."

"Believe me, Ms. Peña, we fight too." He went for a beer. "Can I bring you one?"

"I'm good. Call me Zelda."

"I don't usually tell a tenant she's beautiful. But this one is." He looked at her.

"Thank you, sir. My English is horrible. But I learned since I'm in Brooklyn that 'beauty is skin deep.'"

"Beauty is skin deep for people who have no eyes. You are as beautiful as Cape Cod's winter."

"Mr. Silver Tongue, I hope you will take me to Cape Cod one good day, if we become friends."

"If that is the only promise in my life to keep, that will be it. I will remember how Cinderella looked before she lost her slipper. And, you are my Cinderella."

As I walked in the living room, I said, "The

landlord is here. May I join the American hero and the Venezuelan Cinderella? Hector, have you met Zelda Peña? Zelda, have you met Hector Hedgpine?"

Hector answered. "Stude, we have. Had I known this beauty was here, I would have been here at daybreak."

"And you would have had breakfast with us this morning," Zelda said.

"Stude, your past tenants never cooked your breakfast," Hector said.

"This is a grateful tenant," Zelda answered.

"Are we all ready for Manhattan?" I asked.

"Stude, you didn't tell me to come to go to Manhattan. I will have to use your shirt and pants."

"You know where to find them."

Hector showered, and sang *I've Never Been in Love Before.*

"Stude Bakka, Hector has a lovely voice."

"He is a better pianist; and he is singing a love song for you."

"He is a man of many talents," Zelda said.

"There are other talents you'll soon know." I smiled, looked at her, and she blushed.

In the subway car there was space for three, but I let Hector and Zelda sit together. I sat on another seat and went to bed nodding on a woman's shoulder. When we detrained at Bowling Green, Zelda said, "Stude, you left my shoulder for a strange woman's."

Hector said, "Zelda, Stude's perfume will allow him to sleep on Elizabeth Taylor's shoulder."

"Why didn't you spray some on yourself, Hector, so you could have slept on my shoulder?"

"I did!" Hector exclaimed.

Zelda exclaimed just as quickly. "Hector! Make sure you sleep on my shoulder in the subway when we are going back to Brooklyn."

"Zelda, I will fulfill that promise without fail." Hector looked at her as if they were already mating pals.

We had a wonderful outing in Manhattan. We took pictures with Arturo di Mordica's massive 7,000-pounds-bronze-charging bull that guards 26 Broadway, New York, New York. It signifies the bullish market on Wall Street; and it is the most photographed inanimate object in the world. The crowd that day and everyday speaks for itself. Zelda interpreted for people who only spoke Spanish. Some romanced every part of the bull's body. A woman caressed the bull's balls and compared them with her husband's. Her husband told her, "Honey, I thought my puny size is just good for you, and you cry every time when it's in. Could you imagine if that is in?" He pointed at that.

A little boy went under the bull, held the bull's private part, and called out to his mother in Spanish, "Mama, is here you milk it?"

Zelda answered the kid in Spanish, "Son, this is not a cow."

A man gave Zelda his phone number, and mumbled, "You are so beautiful." She handed his number to Hector. The man smiled and said to Hector, "May I take a picture with your beautiful wife?"

"Sure," Hector said.

We went to Staten Island on the ferry boat and sat at the back. Zelda marveled at the way the concrete jungle of downtown Manhattan with its massive skyscrapers transformed into one solid block of concrete. She asked a passenger to take a picture of three of us. Then I took the camera and shot a picture of Zelda and Hector and kidded:"Please, hug her, Hector. Didn't you tell the man that she's your wife?"

"He said that, not me," Hector snapped back.

"And you said sure," Zelda blurted.

With Hector's hand still on her shoulder, he asked her to show him Brooklyn. She pointed at the spire of One Hanson Place, downtown Brooklyn, near the Long Island Rail Road Terminal. "How do you know that is Brooklyn?"

"I just guess."

"And what is that State across there?"

"New Jersey?"

"Yes, it's New Jersey."

"Would you keep your word if you lose the next bet?" Hector asked.

"Can Stude help me?"

"Take me out of that bet!" I shouted, with a dribbling, spicy hot dog in my mouth, its liquid dropping on my shirt. A tourist interrupted to get photographs with the dwindling New York scenery in the background, and then with 'Lady Liberty' with her lit torch.

Hector resumed with his bet. "Zelda, here is the question. If you lose, you will have to come and spend the day at my place in Park Slope."

"With Stude, of course."

I shouted louder. "Both of you, leave me out of your bets!"

"With or without your landlord," Hector said, and made an eye to me.

"What's the question?" Zelda asked. I could see

she wanted to lose the bet, and to be with him without my presence. He pointed at the Manhattan Bridge and the Brooklyn Bridge. Then he asked to show him Brooklyn Bridge. When she and I walked on the plank of the ferry boat, I'd shown her Brooklyn Bridge. Yet she pointed at the wrong bridge.

"Okay. I will visit your apartment in Park Slope. Would you come with me, Stude Bakka?"

"All my free days are booked for free jazz concerts in Bryant Park."

"I forgot."

She got a job as a waiter in Manhattan, and I suspected she visited Hector after work, but I never asked her about her whereabouts. I did not hear movements upstairs. Her voice was not heard singing songs, in a language that I don't know, when she showered in the morning.

The first hint I got of their romance was the friendship ring on her finger. "Why won't you ask me, Stude Bakka, who gave me this friendship ring?"

"You told me that you are getting plenty tips on your job and you bought a computer. I'm sure it's the tips on your job gave you sufficient money to buy that ring, or one of your *Facebook* friends lent you the money."

"Guess again. If you lose this bet, you will have to edit all my texts to my friends who speak English."

"Why?"

"Most of the waiters are college girls or women waiting on their big break to get on Broadway. I hear them mocking my English and laughing at the way I pronounce words."

"I can help you with your English."

A month later, she asked me, "What's this ring?"

"An engagement ring, of course."

"How do you know?"

"I didn't see you some weekends, and I guess you were with Hector who bought the engagement ring."

"Are you happy for me?"

"Of course, I am!"

"Are you still my best friend and confidant?"

"*Solamente una vez!*"

"Always and forever."

We hugged as happy children awaiting Christmas toys from Santa.

At first, Zelda was Hector's drop-in woman who only stayed for the amount of hours Hector allotted her when he expected other women. She'd come in my room and cry, and I would console her when she put her head on my shoulder. Later on, he called her his 'serious' woman when she slept over on consecutive weekends.

On her return from those consecutive sleepovers, she came to my room singing "He belongs to my heart/Now and forever."

After her tenth-weekend sleepover, he married her, and she was no longer my tenant. I missed her dearly, but I was happy for them because they found joy in each other's company.

3

I was the best man at their wedding, and I advised them to go to Trinidad and Tobago for their honeymoon. In Trinidad, they stayed at the Upside Down Hilton Hotel. On carnival days they paraded in bands and danced to steel band and calypso music on the streets. Zelda matched her movements with the Trinidad women's multi-joint movements and gyrated down to the asphalt.

Hector phoned me and said, "Stude, Trinidad women couldn't out do my wife's waist."

"Hector, no other country's women, not even Brazilian women, could out do Trini women in that department."

They visited the pitch lake, one of the unknown wonders of the world. They stopped by roadside farmers and bought seasoned, boiled corn. They ate the cascadura fish and the cook said when they ordered a second serving, "Those who eat the cascadura in Trinidad have to return to die in Trinidad no matter where they roam."

Both said in unison, "We don't mind dying together in Trinidad or anywhere else if we die together."

In Tobago, they stayed at Crown Point Hotel. They swam like love fishes in Store Bay. Zelda wore her undersized, bright bathing suit swim, bought by Hector, and she relaxed on bath towels by the pool.

He called me from a store in Scarborough, the capital of Tobago. "Stude, I'm reading a *Time Magazine*, but I'm soaking in the admiration that my wife is getting from your men folks."

They went out to sea in a glass-bottomed boat and visited the reefs. They dove to see the undersea kingdom. The boat took them farther out into the ocean and anchored on dry land.

My phone rang, and Hector shouted, "Stude, answer this riddle: Where in the world you can go in the middle of the ocean and walk on dry land?" He hung up without giving me a chance to answer.

Back in Trinidad, he went to play golf and his wife was his caddy.

When they returned from their honeymoon, Zelda came to visit me alone. She said, "Stude, I have a joke for you: A Trini man, a caddy, who was on the green next to us, said aloud so that Hector could hear, 'Whitey, if ah get dat meat, ah go teach you how we eat dat kinda meat down here.'"

Our laughter was riotous.

Hector kept his promise. For their first anniversary, he surprised her with a visit to Cape Cod in the height of winter. She loved it. He hid all her winter gear in his suitcase and gave them to her when they landed. She shouted, "Oh Hector! Oh Hector! This view is lovely beyond words."

"Just as you, honey. You should be on *The Real Hot 100* and on *Maxim*. No part of your body is unruly. People would be buying those magazines by all the airports, only because of you on the magazine covers, my love."

In the second year of their marriage, he kept telling me of her excessive love for texting, and his suspicion of her "having a side piece."

Her grouse was, "His true love has become a burden."

They poured out to me their likes and dislikes for each other. He kept close to me; but Zelda kept closer.

She confessed that she has an appetite for men, and she got that appetite for men from peeping through a keyhole and watching her mother having sex with the Dictator and other men. She also said, she loves to give a man what he wants especially when he gives her his strength of the lower region of his body. She stressed, "Hector isn't one of those men… And you never showed interest in me no matter how I dressed even before I met Hector."

I'd cut her off many times when she wanted to go in details about her sex life with Hector. But when she sent her sex texts for me to edit I was drawn to her language and her knowledge of anatomy and physiognomy.

Every time I asked for Hector, her answer was the same. "With his lover, Betsy. Can we go out and let me bore you with social-media gossips? Gossips, sexting, and posting on *Facebook* keep me alive. I will be picking up the check. My tips are huge, and I flirt with the millionaires after watching how the Broadway wannabes do it."

I was happy to see her. She met me at my job. We went to South Street Seaport, sat outside, and admired the traffic below and on top the Brooklyn Bridge. I pointed, "That's the bridge you lost your bet on."

"Stude Bakka, don't remind me of my deliberate lie to go and sleep with Hector."

We laughed as if we were in the fish market a stone's throw away. She was beautifully dressed and her admirers were many. We had a nice evening eating, drinking, and listening to a singer whose hat was filled with money. She kissed me gently as we parted company.

Our next date when Hector was away on his secret assignment was to the world renown 'Times Square' with its myriads of neon lights, digital commercials half the size of the buildings they are on, people exiting Broadway shows flocking the sidewalks and ignoring the traffic lights. And, of course, the underground businessmen: all the characters of Disney World and the Comic Strips stuck on women and men's faces hustling the passersby to let their children take pictures with them. Square Bob is a favorite with children.

The naked cowboys and cowgirls with guitars on their necks and no music coming from their guitar strings pose for pictures with the tourists. I posed with a woman beautifully painted without bra and fitted in a string bikini. Zelda took our picture and showed the thumb-up sign. I gave the painted woman ten dollars; and Zelda gave her twenty and the fist bump.

We finally sat in the large space on Seventh Avenue. That space was once a fast lane for vehicles heading south to lower Manhattan. It is now landscaped and bounded by Forty Second Street and Fifty Seventh Street. Red chairs and red tables adorn that space on Time Square. We sat and drank non-alcoholic beverages.

"Zee, in the sixties there were a lot of speakeasies in this neighborhood. I remember going into a strip club, and to stay in I had to buy a drink. I bought the cheapest drink—a coke which cost me five dollars. The bouncer put me out because he said I was squeezing my drink."

"Stude, why didn't you buy another coke to stay in to look at the half-naked women climbing on the poles?"

"With my little salary, I couldn't afford to buy another coke for five dollars."

"How does the Good-Morning-America team call Time Square sometimes?"

"I don't know, Zee."

"They call it Social Square."

As we drove in an almost empty subway car to Brooklyn, she asked, "Do you know why a female social-media gossiper is always playing in her wig and kicking out her cramped legs?" She gave me the answer in Spanish; then she spoke in my ear and interpreted what she said in English.

"That's nasty, Zee."

"True! That's how we call those women in the barrio in Venezuela."

"You never lived in the barrio, Zee."

"How the hell you know where I lived, Stude Bakka! You have a knack to disturb me, sometimes, to make me feel like I'm a fool."

"I'm sorry, Zee."

We parted company with our usual embrace and friendly kiss.

I reached home. My phone was ringing off the hook. I thought Zelda was calling to thank me for taking her out. But, it was Hector.

"Stude, who the fuck is Gordon?" His rage came through the phone.

"I don't know him, Hector."

"You know him! You are hiding Zelda's shit from me. You are like my blood brother that I never had. The only difference is your last name is Bakka; and mine is Hedgpine."

"I'm not hiding anything from you, Hector."

"You are close to my wife, more than I'd like

you to be, and I know you know who this fucking *Facebook* Gordon is." He slammed the phone down.

The razor back tickled me in my pocket, and I opened it. In hushed tones, I heard, "Stude Bakka."

"Yes, Zee."

"I'm in trouble. Hector got Gordon's sex text by mistake. His name was above Gordon's, and I touched the wrong name to *send*."

"Who the hell is Gordon?"

"A *Facebook* friend that I send sex text for fun."

"A platonic friend?"

"What that means?"

"A friend like me who is not 'fucking' you while Hector is away risking his life, digging out terrorists from their hiding places for the safety of you, me, and John Public."

She did not answer.

"Up to last night you told me about some of your past lovers but you never told me about Gordon. Are you a 'nymph' — a woman who fucks just for fun?"

She was silent for two minutes.

"Zee, are you there?"

"Yes, I am here "

"Is Gordon someone you had introduced me

to?"

"No, Stude Bakka."

"You are sure he's not your 'new' lover?" I used the adjective 'new' to see if I could elicit new information, but her English was improved, and she was aware of my connotation 'new' in the degree of comparison that I used to trap her lies.

"Yes, I'm sure. The only recent lover that I had was Mary. We ended our relationship because I didn't have the money to help her pay the rent, and I refused to beg anybody for favors. You are the first and only person in my life that I've asked for a favor. And that is the very week that you took me in without money to pay your rent. I have no 'new', lover." She stressed the word 'new.'

"Where's Hector?"

"He left the house in a rage."

"You know he has a licensed revolver?"

"Yes."

"He ever threatened you with it?"

"No. I have a gun too. I had stolen it from David when I ran away from him because he had promised 'as the sun comes out tomorrow that he'd kill me if he suspects that a man fucks me.' I'd told him that I'd never let a man tell me what I can, or cannot do, with my body—married or unmarried."

"You never told me you have a gun?"

She did not answer.

"Zee, you know where Hector keeps his gun?"

"Yes."

"See if it is there." I heard her groan.

"It is not there."

"You know where he went?"

"He left here cursing me and calling me a whore."

"Zee, I'm happy."

"What! What!"

"If he were calm, then it would have been dangerous for you. Hector has his father's disposition. Hector's father was cool as a cucumber, but as calm as his father was, he murdered his mother because of her infidelity. I'm going to find Hector."

"Thanks."

"Who is Gordon?"

She equivocated. I hung up, and left to find Hector.

I met Hector at our friend, Gabby. They were chatting and drinking beers. I joined in. I did not know if Hector had his gun, but I knew he was mourning for Betsy who had just died. Hector is a decoy with Homeland Security, and Betsy was his pal who searched for bombs left by terrorists after the Twin Towers were first bombed.

He wore a black band on his left arm. I'd asked him once why the band is on his left arm. He said, if he put the band on his right arm he was likely to forgive, and forgiveness was not his motto.

Betsy was his black Labrador that died from a terrorist's bomb. She had high energy, speed, stamina, charisma, and the sense of humans. She was one of five dogs used as evidence in court against terrorists. She was bred in North Carolina, and the original dog breeder refused to divulge Betsy's pedigree to anyone except Homeland Security.

The only information the dog breeder told people about Betsy was: She loves French fries from Wendy's. And she knows the difference if someone slips a single McDonald's fry in her meal. She would eat every fry except that single McDonald's.

Even though I suspected Hector hated his job, I never discussed that her husband wanted to leave his job because he was not compensated sufficiently for the damages he suffered in his leg. In fact, I will never tell him what she tells me, and I will never tell her what he tells me.

I know from experience when a husband and wife close their bedroom door and each feels the warmth from each other's body, they become small minds and discuss people; and their discussions of newsmongers become their foreplay.

Hector, Gabby, and I knocked glasses, and we sang our theme song: *One for three, three for one, and nobody else.* Hector and I parted company without saying a word to each other.

Many years ago, he had told me, when we were discussing men and women's infidelity, he had said, "I love every inch of my wife's body, and I'll kill for it."

I called Zelda. "Zee, he's on his way home. Make sure you are temptingly dressed. You are his wife; but I know his moods."

"Okay. Did he tell you what happened between us?"

"Don't bother. You will be fine. Don't turn your back on him to sleep tonight no matter how loud he snores."

"You are my Angel from the day we met. And don't forget to introduce me to your new woman if I live to see tomorrow."

"You will live. And don't forget when you go on your cell to look carefully at the name written before you press the 'send' button. I know you like sexting to playfully turn men on, but stay away from doing that when Hector is home during these precious days that you are alive. Let him alone enjoy your goodies."

"Last night he had the goodies, and he sang along with Kurt Elling, the 2000 Down Beat Male Vocalist, on the TV, *A Home is Not a Home*, and he added his own lyrics: 'Unless Zelda is there/ Stay in love with me, Zelda/ for forever and ever.' The way he looked at me when he sang the words, 'forever and ever,' I was overcome with fear."

A week later my cell displayed her name, and I opened the text. It was the full sex text she had sent, by mistake, to her husband, instead of to Gordon. I wondered why she sent that letter to me, too.

Before I read the full text, I called Zelda. "Zee, why you sent this text to me?"

She answered: "Read it:"

Gordon, I came to New York at age 19, but now I am 24. It took me five years before I told anyone— man or woman—I love you. I love you, Gordon, from the minute my eyes met yours. At first I thought it was the dust in my eyes that caused me to look in your direction. You may never guess where I first saw you, and how I got your Facebook address. But that is not important now. What is important is that I love you from the moment I saw you.

You were sitting with a woman in the Literature Section on the first floor of the Brooklyn Library at Grand Army Plaza. You were sitting under Norman Mailer's large, molded photograph on the southern wall. You were facing me, and I could have looked into your eyes. The color of your eyes is as blue as Frank Sinatra's. Oh how I love them and would look into them every moment of the day if you were mine. But for some reason or reasons 'that' woman who was sitting with you exchanged her seat for yours. Now you were sitting with your back facing me up to the time that both of you left the library. And 'that' woman gave me the stink eye, and I gave her my middle finger as far as I could have pushed it up her stink arse.

Many nights I have gone to bed knowing 'that' selfish bitch purposely exchanged her seat with yours. And she did that to end my feelings for you—feelings that she felt would have traveled from me as fast as lightning, but those feelings are still with me. Since then, I have been going to the Brooklyn Library to get literature for immigrants' knowledge, and I sit at the same table, on the same chair facing Norman Mailer's pic, hoping you'd come one day alone before I got married. If you had come and held my hand in the most casual way I would not have got married.

I have a wonderful husband. His name is Hector, and he works for Homeland Security. He never tells me what he does, neither where he goes. He only speaks of his pal, Betsy, a dead dog, which was in a higher rank than he; and that dog could have tell if a crook had false money in a bag for Hector to notify the authorities. Hector will stay in the background when the arrest was made. The first time that I heard that some dogs are in a higher rank than their trainers was when he told me. Hector and I had lots of laughter about his inferiority, not to me, but something with a female name; but it was his dog. I believe that Betsy was of a higher rank than my heroic husband when Betsy gave up her life for her inferior—my husband.

I, too, will give up my life for you because I've read your Post and your description of the indigenous life in the barrios in Spain and your help to the people there. I visited a boy in the barrio in Caracas named Pedro, and I will tell you about him if we meet one day. My mother writes me begging me to come back home because her health is failing. But I have a great feeling that she misses me more than her report of her failing health.

I love Brooklyn and its disheveled look; and I love seeing roaches walking on the walls because I've never seen that in my life of luxury in my parents' home. I feel at home when I'm with Mexicans and Colombians. I don't care for Cubans. They think they are too cultured, too educated, and too sophisticated to be grouped with us.

Ever since Betsy gave up her life to a terrorist's bomb and saved my husband, my husband has not been the same. No romance! No sex! Once I knew where he kept his gun. Now I don't. I love him, but he does not return my love or my gestures that resemble love.

These days I feel like a sixteen year old who was never kissed. And when I was kissed and had sex at seventeen with Pedro, I was very happy. He wasn't afraid of the Dictator, who was my father's friend, who would have killed him because the Dictator had his dirty eyes on me.

Pedro taught me boy sex. Now I long for sex from a man like you. I hate the word 'sex.' 'Fuck' is more sincere as a noun than as a verb. And that is what I need now—a good fuck from you to make me scream. I want us to make music on each other's body just the way I'm dreaming of doing it with you. I hope *my dream comes true.*

I'm going to prepare Hector's dinner. When can we meet? ZH.

Somehow, I was glad when the text ended. I now had a new problem: Should I tell Hector that she sent me a copy of the text? To eradicate that thought I made a sandwich as big as Dagwood's. I pulled out the long Italian bread from the bag on the kitchen counter and cut it with the knife I had never used. The steel blade that cut the bread was as sharp as a razor. I looked at the blade carefully when I pulled it out of the long box. I washed it under hot water poured from the kettle, dried it, and sliced the Italian dough in half but did not let the halves separate. I jammed one half to the ceramic wall. In went hard salami over Swiss and American cheeses, followed with sliced tomatoes. Then ham under salsa pepper sauce was rammed in. I hate Mayo, but I put a little and rubbed it over ketchup and the mixture became mauve. I had bought that knife over thirty years ago from Sears Roebuck on Bedford Avenue in Brooklyn as a present for a dear friend named Carmen, but I lost her address and her friendship.

Carmen married a Haitian businessman be-cause I didn't escort her to a party in East New York.

I knew I would be safe in East New York because she had introduced me to her uncle, and she was proud to tell me, "Stude, he's a mafia and had sworn to the Oath of Omerta."

I was searching for a hook for a book I was writing, and getting that hook was more important than escorting Carmen to a party. An editor of repute had told me if I get a hook for my book that he likes, he may consider reading it; otherwise, he'll be throwing my book in the flush pile. I said in a sad voice, "Carmen, go to the party without me tonight because I'm expecting a long distance call from overseas, and it is very important." She went without me, and met her husband there. I had seen the pastel-colored dress she wore at the party with more holes than cloth.

A buzzing fly flew by, and I covered the Italian with five leaves of paper towel. The phone rang.

"Hello."

"Did you read it, Stude Bakka?"

"Yes, Zee; but hastily."

"You have time to talk?"

"I'm turning an Italian into a Dagwood's."

"Can I come over to get the bigger half? Don't tell me two halves are equal. I don't know much English, but I know enough to bargain."

"Where is your husband?"

"With Homeland on a big tip off."

"What kind of tip off?"

"You know he will never tell. Since Betsy was killed he doesn't trust his shadow. Neither does he trust mine since he read my text."

"I'm not finished plugging my Italian, but I want to bite her in the belly without sharing her bottom."

"I'm coming to eat her bottom."

"My woman is on the way."

"An Italian?"

"That's not your business."

"I don't care. I'll be right over."

Her Volkswagen came to a screeching halt. The door was opened; she ran into the kitchen and washed her hands.

"Zee, since you were living here, you know I do not let people wash their hands in my kitchen sink."

She ignored me and took over my kitchen. She heated the already cooked boneless-Alaska baccalao, and poured it into my Dagwood's with sliced onions and olives. She cut the sandwich in half, and rammed in crushed avocado.

"Stude, I'm your guest, so I'm choosing first."

"By the way, is Gordon white?"

"He is vanilla."

"What's the difference between white and vanilla?"

"One is a WASP; one is white Hispanic. I know the difference because my father and the Dictator always argued about who is of the Western Anglo Saxon People and who is Hispanic.

My mother would join the argument and say, 'I'm 'Bob' a/k/a Black-on-Black.'"

We measured our halves, and they were even to the crumbs.

A new conversation began.

"Stude Bakka, could you remember what I told you when we first met in Pizza Hut?"

"I remember. I know that is not the question you came to ask me."

"Stude, if you were a woman….?"

I looked at her and opened my eyes wide.

"And your husband was always away; you never knew where he was; and when he is coming home, would you take a chance?"

"What kind of chance?"

"Any kind of chance?"

"*Any* is too broad."

"When you took me in, many nights I came to your room to pour out my past life but you stopped me and never gave me a chance to speak of my first husband. David's hurt is deep, and I want to talk about it today. I'm comfortable telling you things than telling Hector. Today I'm going to tell you what kind of chance."

I nodded with a blank face, but when she spoke I was seeing her past life. It was as if I were on the spot when David Ide had his boots on her.

"David and I had a civil wedding with no family in attendance. We were 'love-fuckers,' never friends, and were married in the space of one month from the day we met. We lived for two years and seven months. We lived seven different places before we parted; and eventually I got my divorce in Las Vegas."

"Why you moved to so many places?"

"I want you to just listen. If you ask me questions, I will break down and cry. You can tell Hector things that I hadn't the guts to tell him, and why I want him to show me love rather than give all his love to a dead dog and to his Homeland Security job.

"I had come to this country from Venezuela only knowing a couple verbs and nouns in English and landed in Brooklyn. I hadn't friends or family here. I was an illegal alien and afraid that Immigration will find me. Every policeman I saw on the beat, I thought he was looking for me to deport me because my father and his Dictator friend paid them handsomely to find me.

"This was my daily fear. It made me so sick, that I lost my thickness from one hundred and forty pounds to one hundred and nineteen pounds, but I like my new size with my broad hips because my body remains firm.

"My body remains firm because I walked the streets for many hours because I lived at a girlfriend but she never gave me keys to her apartment. So I walked Brooklyn streets until she came home at crazy, odd hours and opened her door for me to go in.

"Walking one day, I saw a shadow. I thought it was an Immigration policeman following me. But it was not an Immigration policeman. A soothing voice said, 'Hello,' when our shoulders touched. I don't know if I touched his shoulder from fear that shifted my balance to his shoulder, or, if he made his shoulder touch mine to start a conversation.

"From his accent, I knew he was Hispanic, and from the Dominican Republic because I know a DR's accent in my sleep. My mother had many DRs as house keepers. But he refused to speak Spanish.

"Hello, I answered, wondering if my pronunciation were correct, even though my English had improved somewhat. I took the courage to look at him and knew he was not a man of the law because I knew a law man by his gait, his appearance, and when he disguises himself as a homeless man, I can pick him out blindfolded. This stranger probably read my mind, heard the rumbling in my belly, knew that I was hungry, and penniless in my discolored purse to buy breakfast."

He said, "Would you believe I saw you last week on this block, and I was praying to meet you here again."

"Where on this block? I looked at him and smiled seductively."

"I can't remember the exact spot, but I never forget a face, especially one as beautiful as yours."

"If I could speak English as good as you, I would say…What is the word when you don't believe a person?"

"You are a liar."

"Both of us smiled. And he spoke first."

"My name is David Wilkes. I will be honored if

you have breakfast with me."

"My name is Zelda Peña, but my friends call me Zee. He held my arm and led me inside the diner; and I made myself accessible for his firm grip. He pulled out my seat. I sat quickly because I was ready to eat a crow left by a bird of condor.

"Before he sat, the waiter came to him, and he told the waiter, 'Rick, the same for two.' Whatever it was, I was going to devour it. Everything was in my favor because the waiter brought our breakfast in seven minutes: toast, butter, scrambled eggs, sausage, marmalade, coffee, six packs of sugar, six servings of milk, orange juice, a jug of water, and two glasses."

"My name is David Ide," he said.

"I remembered he first introduced his last name as Wilkes, but I did not ask him why he changed his last name from Wilkes to Ide because my hunger dictated the length of my conversation.

"He touched my hand and said, 'I always say a silent prayer before each meal.'

"He sounded like my mother's pastor in Caracas who says the same thing. My mother liked her pastor and always invited him for dinner. In my mother's absence, he came and sat next to me and tried to put his hands under my dress when the servants were not serving us. He stopped coming to dine with us when I threatened that I will tell the Dictator.

"David bent his head, and I bent mine. I pulled my feet below the table, and hid my scaling nail polish and ugly toes that needed a pedicure months ago."

"I enjoyed this breakfast with you Zelda. I hope we meet again," he said.

"Sure, I shouted, because my hunger was gone; and I had the strength to shout aloud."

I looked at her and asked, "Zee, weren't you distrustful of a man who gave himself two different last names before breakfast ended?"

"Yes, Stude Bakka. Hunger was my master, and I obeyed her."

"I never knew 'Hunger' is feminine gender." We laughed.

I bit my Dagwood, and I shook my head as Colombo in his dirty raincoat.

"Stude Bakka, up to this day I believe I married David because he ended my hunger that morning."

I saw her deep sorrow, and I tried to end her sadness with humor. "If you finish your Dagwood first, help me with mine."

She didn't take my bait. She continued to pour out her sadness with the man who ended her hunger.

"I could not get good jobs because I couldn't speak good enough to be understood when I was interviewed for a better job. I got a job at a factory doing odd things. I stood in the assembly line for six hours daily. One hour for lunch break. It was the first time in my life that I knew what some workers do for a living, and making money was not easy for illegal immigrants in America.

"I never saw my husband until two months after he paid the first rent. For the other months I had to pay the rental of $13.25 weekly, and most times I hadn't the rent because I borrowed money in advance from an aged woman in the factory to buy bread; and I boiled lettuce to eat with my bread. The week I expected the out-of-town landlord will come for his rent, I never turned on the lights. I lived in darkness for that week.

"David walked into the dark room unexpectedly one night and spoke softly, 'Pack up. Don't turn on the lights.'"

"Why?" He slapped me so hard that I felt the blow in my spine.

"Bitch, when I say something do it without questioning me." He smelled like if he drank a keg of cheap rum.

Her eyes flooded. She put down her sandwich; I put down mine; and then she spoke after two minutes.

"That was my first move from Brooklyn to Newark, New Jersey. I will skip my second, third, fourth, fifth, and sixth moves, and go to my seventh."

As Zelda spoke, she reminded me of my life in Fyzabad barracks and the treatment of barracks women by their husbands or man friends. She saw that my mind was straying from listening to her true story, so she called my full name to get my attention.

"Stude Bakka, I want you to slap this ear."

"I indulge in love, not in domestic violence."

"Just hit it." She looked at me sternly. "Hit it hard!"

I hit it, but not hard.

"Harder," she said.

I did.

"Do you think I felt it?"

"Of course!"

"I don't know the difference with pain and no pain on that part of my body. It is numb."

Then her face took a different countenance before she spoke.

"I was living in Philadelphia. David left in his

car. Before he left, he unplugged the black-and-white TV and put it in his car. He left a week before the rent was due. He left me as when he first saw me—hungry and without money to pay the rent. I had another assembly-line job at a factory putting radio parts together, and even though the snow was high to my knees, and I had no boots, I always leave my job at lunch time and go walking through the snow because I had nothing to eat.

"I didn't want the other employees to notice my plight each day. My boss, Simon, blocked me one day and led me to the lunchroom. He bought lunch for both of us. His kindness went on for two and a half months, and he gave me overtime so that I can buy a pair of boots.

"I stopped hiding from the landlord because I was able to pay the rent of $13.25 weekly. The landlord smiled when he came for his rent and the room was not in darkness. He wrote the receipt for the full rental of $13.25, and he gave me back one dollar; and my 'many thanks' to him made him uncomfortable.

"With the little money that I'd saved, I bought nice dishes and pots for the kitchen. Stude Bakka, I'm not boasting, but I came from a family with plenty. I am an only child, and the Dictator supplied a car with an official plate and a chauffeur for me whenever I wished one. So I dressed up my little room as if I still lived a luxurious life and expected the Dictator who came to see my mother, his lover."

"Zee, you never told me the Dictator's name." The way she looked at me, I knew that question did not fall within the ambit of my business so I shut up.

"I shopped and prepared a sumptuous dinner and invited Simon to dine with me. He came nicely dressed; and I was dressed scantily to greet him. The perfume on the sexual parts of my body was the same my mother used when she expected the Dictator."

"This table is for me?"

"You deserve more than this, Simon."

I looked at her as if I knew what would follow in her sad story, but I never knew she would be so blunt to tell me such pieces of her life. When she was vulgar, she was vulgar, and meant to be vulgar in sex to show the fire that burned within her body.

"Stude Bakka, I don't know if it was the effect of the two bottles of wine we drank, but Simon and I fucked on the floor, on the twin bed with new sheets, and on the two chairs that I covered with clean pillow cases. I enjoyed every part of his body, and he enjoyed mine more.

"I begged Simon to stay to show him the different ways I fucked with Pedro and Carlos in the barrio to prevent me from getting pregnant. I learned that in boarding school. In boarding school one of the girls told me she likes people to look at her when she's doing it, and why can't both of us do it for fun.

"I wanted to show Simon what I learned by peeping through a keyhole in my parents' house.

"Through that keyhole I saw what the Dictator did to and for my mother, and what she did to and for him. My mother knew I was peeping through the keyhole because she had caught me before.

"When we spoke about it, she said, 'Badzee, if it satisfies you by peeping, go-ahead; but don't take him away from me. I know he is in love with you, and he teaches you how to use guns and shoot guns on his private range. I'd rather you go away and do what I do, but not here.

"My mother was a good wife to my father but a nymph for the Dictator and other men. Both the Dictator and my mother were kinky lovers. She called him 'Wasp,' and he called her 'Bob.'

"She told him of all the men who had sex with her, called their names, how they did it, and forced him to do it as they did it. Telling a man about another man turned her on; and it does the same to me. But Hector forbids me of talking about another man when we are having sex.

"When the Wasp and Bob were finished having fun, they had supper with my father; and I'd asked the Wasp to let his chauffeur drop me to see my girlfriend. I never let the chauffeur drop me in front of Pedro or Carlos' broken-down shacks in the barrio.

"After my happy moments with the boys, I'd call the Wasp to let his chauffeur come back for me. When I returned home the Wasp would leave. I'd play the piano, and my mother and father would dance to *Solamente una vez* in a Latin beat.

"My father was thirty years older than my mother, and he loved her dearly. My father is a doctor but he no longer practices medicine. At twelve years old, I was sensible enough to know that my father knew my mother had lovers, and my mother's lovers always brought expensive gifts for me. I convinced myself that I, too, will have many lovers to bring me gifts. Not you, Stude Bakka." She smiled.

"Zee, I love Hector, but yours is a friendship that I'll always cherish. You treat me as your therapist."

"Stude, believe it or not, you are my therapist without a fee. There's something about you that I've read in Matthew 25: You took me in when I was homeless. You fed me when I was hungry.... Let me go back to my time with Simon before I cry over you. After Simon and I drained the wine bottles, we had sex again, and he refused to shower. He was so eager to leave that he didn't kiss me goodbye.

"He shook my hand very businesslike as when he interviewed me for the job in his father's factory. He told me, he loves my body, and he loves bi-racial women. I begged him endlessly to sleepover. He said although I had not seen David for many months, he could walk in any time because this room is his castle. I am David's wife; and David would be within his right to kill him. I told Simon David would kill both of us.

"While he was dressing and my wanting to admire his physique and to delay him, I told him how I came to New York. I talked about Carlos, my last lover in Caracas, who risked his life and limb. He helped in my planning to run away from home because the Dictator had me in mind to be his lover. Carlos and I knew after the Dictator was tired with my mother, and I objected to going to bed with the Dictator, one of his henchmen would kill me and make it look as an accident.

"The day before I left, Carlos and I staged a cursing and a hatred for each other around the dinner table in front of my parents and the Dictator. We did that so that nobody would suspect that Carlos knew of my plans in case our plans were discovered.

"My mother knew my plans, and she wanted me to leave.   Late in the night when my father was fast asleep, my mother and I read the Bible. We prayed to Mary, and we cried. My mother begged me to come home before she dies, and I told her when I get married in America my husband and I will come to see her and my father at a place unknown to the Dictator. Mother's smile cheered me up, and both of us wiped our tears.

"I held on to Simon and had my perfumed breasts in his face, but he pushed me away and shouted, 'I won't stay! I won't stay!' He rushed out of my room and drove off in his car. I could smell the burnt smell from his tires.

"I left the dinner table set for two new lovers with two empty wine bottles, all the dirty dishes, and all the dirty towels strewn all over the room. I could still smell Simon's masculinity on the sheets. His smell turned me on, and I enjoyed my body with my fingers. It was as if he was still on me and doing all those kinky things that I'd learned by peeping through the keyhole."

Somehow I foresaw the ending of the *Zelda Ide Story*, but it was more than I wanted to hear.

"Stude Bakka, I went to bed in a fetal pose with my right ear up. The blow from David's fist threw me off the bed. Up to this day I cannot hear a thing in this ear. He kicked me like a football. His body was rank. He pushed my face between his legs, and I had to do what he commanded me to do.

"Then he went and crushed a white stuff in his special bowl with a sharp blade. He sniffed the white stuff until the bowl was empty.

"At that time, I did not know that white stuff was cocaine; but I knew he had little bags of them. When people came for them, he'd put me behind the folding blind in the room and tell me, 'Don't come out until I tell you.'"

I looked at her and tried to hide my tears. "Zee, if I were a woman with a druggy husband like David who only cared for himself, his cocaine, his cocaine friends, and he always left me hungry, I, too, would have taken a chance to get food to appease my hunger. And I'm glad Simon had the sense of King Solomon and knew when to leave no matter how good is the Venezuelan goodie. Is it that good?"

"Yes." She shook her head.

We measured the remaining Dagwood in our hands, and we burst out laughing as happy kids who think the world is theirs and theirs only.

4

"Love is a many *splintered* thing," Hector said.

"Why you said that?"

"My love for Zelda should be splendored, but it is not. I love her with every drop of my blood, but I'm having bad vibes about her."

"Like what?"

"You are my best friend, and I get the feeling you are hiding stuff that I should know about my wife."

"Like what?"

"Why did you come over to meet me at Gabby's house the night I left home with my gun?"

"Gabby is our mutual friend, and I go to look for her pretty often, even when you are not around. You can call and ask her."

"You want me to believe that?"

"Why shouldn't you?"

"I'm having a beer. Bring one for you?"

Before I put the beer to my mouth, he spoke.

"Who's Gordon?"

"Gordon who?"

"Social-media Gordon."

"Someone has that name?" I asked.

"Yes. That's in *Facebook* and his code name for his cell."

"My computer is down."

"But yet you advised my wife on how to answer my question of 'Who is Gordon?'"

"Me?"

"You thought I would kill her for the terrorist who killed Betsy after I read her sex text to him. I had walked with my gun that night because I didn't trust her. I never trusted her. I knew she never trusted a man after what her first husband did to her. I'd let her hold my gun many times when there were no bullets in it. The way she handled my revolver and spun it like John Wayne, I could see she's accustomed to holding, playing, and firing all kinds of guns. Homeland Security taught me a lot about pretenders."

I kept silent.

"I'm her husband, but she prefers to confide in you. Why?"

I ignored his question and asked, "What her

first husband did to her?"

"Didn't she tell you how she got away from him after he beat her like if he were beating a cobra? Her type is a cobra."

I kept silent.

"Didn't she tell you, her confidant, what her first husband did to her when he came home after two or three months, and he saw her table decorated with fine china and two empty wine bottles?"

"Bits and pieces of her story."

"After he beat and kicked her up, he tested her love for him."

"How?"

"He took her to his favorite club where he took other women, and he asked the DJ to play *Put Your Head on My Shoulder.* She put her head on his shoulder, grind on him the Latin way, and they moved their bodies suggestively to slow, sex-making music."

I couldn't wait for Hector to finish. "And?"

"As soon as they got home he wailed her body with his belt buckle, and he told her, 'Bitch, I beat you up last night and tonight you rested your head on my shoulder as if I were the lover you had fucked with on my bed last night.' She went on her knees and begged for mercy; and she had to do whatever he asked her to do, sexually.

"Stude, I told you before that I left the Army to join Homeland, and in my job I know what illegal aliens go through to stay in this country. Zelda, like many others who had great lives in their country, thought the grass is greener in America. She did not know this country has laws to protect battered women. All she knew was she wanted to be legal in America, and David gave her that legal status.

"Now she's very astute, and she knows America's laws and where to go for help. Without provocation, she told me she will hurt any man even if he's in fits enjoying organism and he pulls her hair hard when they are making love. Her favorite line is 'Judas walked with Jesus, and I wouldn't be Jesus-like and turn the other cheek.'"

I chuckled.

"Stude, talk the truth. Why you came to Gabby's house that night?"

Zelda walked in. "Hi, guys, you are talking about me?" She kissed her husband on his lips as softly as the drop of a dewdrop, and she kissed my cheek as if I were her old uncle who bought the ugliest doll for her at Christmas.

"We are talking about the way you look, Zelda,"

Hector said.

"Spanx is in. You like it on me?"

"Sure, sure!" Hector rubbed her bottom. "It's better than Kim Kardashian's."

"I know. I bought dinner."

"Enough for me?" I asked.

"Stude, I still have some of my Venezuelan habits. My mother always had sufficient food for two extra mouths and her servants." She shared the dinner, and we had great fun.

I spent the evening looking at Hector and his wife and knew that a family that lives in harmony is a happy family. And Judas with Jesus was a wonderful duo until Judas kissed Jesus. My mother always said, "Stude, teeth and tongue live in the same house, and they will have fun and clash sometimes." And so it was with Zelda, Hector, and me.

After we ate our dinner, we moved the furniture and danced. Hector's dance moves surprised me. He's good. I danced to calypso music and took off my shirt and waved it as if I'm in a J'ouvert carnival band in Trinidad and Tobago. The only things missing were two women under each arm.

Hector and Zelda held a broom, and they told me to limbo under the broom as low as I could. Then

Hector and I held a broom for Zelda to limbo below it as low as possible. I had never seen such artistry of a woman's body gyrating below a pole.

We were tired, and we rested. Then we had a new kind of energy for discussing fashions, the jeweled chain around Jay Z's neck, and whether Jennifer Lopez and Kim Kardashian's arses are real.

I was shocked when Zelda turned the discussion into politics. "The first job of any politician is how to stay as long as possible in office. That's how it is in Venezuela, and that's how it is for the thief with the biggest bag in America."

"Where you learned that, Zee," I asked.

"I learned that in Caracas from the Dictator, my friend."

"She learned that from me!" Hector shouted.

Zelda changed the subject again. "You are always trying to decode my password."

"Me!" Hector screamed.

"Most times you treat me as if I were the terrorist's bomb that killed Betsy."

"Zelda, don't go there." Hector pointed at her.

I interrupted. "Let's have some music, Hector." I wet four sheets of paper towel, wiped his fingers, and led him to the keyboard.

"Zee, you will play after. Do you know Hector and I went to Jazz Mobile in Harlem, had some of the best teachers in the seventies, and I am jealous of Hector's improvisation as Billy Taylor's? Billy Taylor was one of our teachers. He was a phenomenal pianist."

I looked at Hector. "I want you to play any tune in the style of the 1950's keyboardist like Joe Alterman."

"Which one?" Hector smiled.

"Anyone that Betsy liked when both of you relaxed after a hard day's work."

Hector played his composition, *Betsy, Where Are You Now?*   He cried aloud, packed his bag, and said, "I'm leaving."

"Do you have to leave tonight, Hector?" I asked.

"Stude, you can sleepover with her." He pointed at his wife.

"Hector, I have a bed where I live."

I left with him. "Hector, you have to curb your temper. Betsy is already dead."

"And I don't mind dying now," he said.

Hector went away on a private investigation.

Zelda was promoted to Cashier in the restaurant. The restaurant was remodeled. Zelda dressed as an executive and rushed to her English classes twice weekly. She could not wait to be home to get on her favorite instrument—her computer, to meet *Facebook* buddies. I had asked her how she picks *Facebook* friends.

"I pick them if I like the sound of their names."

"Do all of them give their right names, birth dates, and occupations?"

"Hell, no! If he says his name is The Mark of Zorro, I'll know he's bullshitting me; but if he says his name is Zorro Zorro, I'll believe him. I know a singer named William Williams, and in France I had met a Frenchman named Pierre Pierre."

"So you will communicate on *Facebook* with a man named Zorro Zorro."

"Sure!"

"How would you address him in a sex text?"

"Hi, Zorro Zorro, my name is May May. My favorite sport is digging for worms for bait to go fishing."

I looked at her as I look at liars.

"Why are you looking at me like that, Stude Bakka?"

"That's the way Hector looked at me when I lied and told him that I didn't know who Gordon is and your relationship with him."

"He asked you that?"

"Yes. And he also knew when I dropped by Gabby's pad, I did not come to see Gabby but to check on his temper."

She was not shocked to know that her husband can read not only between the lines but over and under them. I could see that she was comparing the past with her first husband, David, and the present with Hector.

She came off her computer and said, "Hector slapped me gently when we were having sex, and I warned him, only do that to me if I do that to him. That bastard, David, used to tie me loosely to the bed post and leave me. Dumb me unloosened myself and tried to run away not knowing he was outside waiting. He'd beat me, and I never loosened the rope again."

"When did you get the chance to run away?"

"I'll never tell a man what I did."

"An old girlfriend tells me women's secrets."

"Take it from me, Stude, she'll never tell you everything."

"When I worked at Chase Manhattan Bank as a Trouble Man, handled items in difficulty, and spoke to the Traders, Habib, my Arab friend, was telling Sarah, the Jewish woman, a certain man's secret; and I was pissed to know he was divulging that secret."

"That was a long time ago, so you can tell me."

"Habib had two dates—one with a Palestinian woman, the other an Israeli—for seven o' clock in the evening. He picked up Date Number 1 at 5 pm . He drove her around and made love to her in his car till six. He pretended he couldn't get his car started. He came out of the car, opened the bonnet, touched different parts of the engine, and cursed the car for not starting to take out Date Number 1 to a motel. He flagged down a taxi; gave Date Number 1 the money he had to take her to the motel; told her to get home safely; he's going to call his mechanic to fix the car; and he will drop by later to see her. When Date Number 1 left, he drove off happily and picked up Date Number 2 on the stroke of seven o' clock."

"Stude Bakka, that Arab couldn't try that shit on me."

"I guess so."

Hector came home after two weeks, and he invited me for dinner. He and I hugged and I could feel his joy in seeing me, the same way as when we first became friends.

We became friends in the strangest of ways. I

was in a coffee shop talking to myself, and blaming myself for losing my job because I was concentrating too much on the new book I was drafting instead of doing my secretarial work efficiently at the law firm of Sage Gray Todd & Sims.

He tapped me on my shoulder and said, "Brother, I can give you a loan and wait until you make it big with your name in neon lights on Broadway."

"Oh my God ! You heard me?"

"Yes, brother. I'm Hector Hedgpine. How much do you need?"

"I'm Stude Bakka. I'm expecting my unemployment check this week. Whatever you can loan me, I'd grab it. I expect a better job with another Wall Street law firm."

This time as we ended our embrace, he said, "My wife has four thousand friends on *Facebook.*"

"Did she tell you about Zorro Zorro?"

We laughed.

"I'm finished cooking. Guys, come and eat," Zelda said.

"Zee, I hope it is not that Venezuela molé again," I said.

"Stude Bakka, neither am I serving you Trinidad and Tobago callaloo. How do you people eat that slimy food, full of okras and spinach beaten into a mush?"

"You came from Caracas. How do you know so much about Trini's cooking?"

"My father and his brother, Caesar, had the best known fishing fleet in Venezuela. They rescued many of your people when they came into our country late at nights in the traffickers' boats at the height of the contraband trade. Those poor people from your country did not know where to go when they were put ashore by the traffickers who took their money and sailed away."

"Up to this day the Government of Venezuela is still trying to shift Trinidad and Tobago's sea boundary for their fishing trade just in the same way as they are trying to steal Guyana's jungle."

"Both of you, please, stop reproaching each other. Let's eat," Hector said. "Zelda, let me say the Grace Before Meal in Spanish to show our visitor who is learning to speak Haitian *Kreyol* how improved is my Spanish since my loving wife became my teacher. Did he tell you about his Haitian woman named Bebe?"

"Zee, Bebe will tell you 'Haiti is the only successful revolt in the history of the world.' She read that

to me in a book about Haiti written by Laurent Du-
Bois."

"Stude, tell me something about what your
woman told you about that voodoo stuff?"

"Zee, you are very ethnocentric. You think
your Hail Mary religion is better than other people's.
Haiti, the land of mountains, has a lot of herbalist
healers. Hougan is a good Voodoo priest; Bokor is
an evil one. Haiti has a good story to tell the world.
Since 1804 that Black Country won its Independence
from France. Thousands of Americans do not know
Haitians helped the Americans in their fight for independence in Savannah, Georgia."

"Whom does Bebe worship with—the Hougan
priest or the Bokor priest?"

"I will tell you, if you tell us who Gordon is?"

Zelda looked at me with her stink eye. Hector,
her Homeland Security husband, changed the subject. We were relaxing in the den. She wore no bra in
a tight see-through top, and her nipples pointed at us.

Hector said, "Zelda, don't believe a word that
agnostic said about anything. He needs to write a
book about baby food, how to mix crushed potato
with butter, and how to put guacamole in the baby
mixture when the baby is one year old."

Zelda was not confused with Hector's baby talk and baby formula. She knew he wanted to make her feel comfortable and take her mind away from the name "Gordon" as part of the dinner discourse. She, too, had her way of changing the conversation and telling her husband what would interest him.

"Honey," she moved close to her husband, "late one night traveling on the 'A' train, I sat near a guy who was reading some loose papers written in Spanish on how to make a bomb."

"What kind of guy?" Hector asked before her sentence ended.

"Just a guy."

"How does he look? Describe him."

"I am not going to do that."

"Why?"

"Since you joined Homeland Security you think everyone resembling those people is a terrorist."

"You are judging me, Zelda Hedgpine?" He was very angry.

I interrupted. "I forgot to tell both of you Austin Tuitt, better known as Elder T, for his community work in Brooklyn, will be speaking about the United Peoples Inclusive Flag to be launched and hoisted in May 2016. I told him that I will be bringing both of you to hear about launching the flag in 2016."

Still angry, Hector shouted, "Why is Elder T going to fly a new flag on American soil? Is he anti-American?"

"I don't think so. He says the United Peoples Inclusive Flag emerges from recognition that national flags do not represent the people from grass root up. National flags represent the elite-minority group that manages and hoodwinks the masses; but the United Peoples Inclusive Flag represents the peoples rallying emblem from grass root up."

"I'll go to hear Elder T on my day off."

When Zelda left the table, he said, "I will catch that nymph and her man in my bed. She thinks her bag of tricks is better than mine."

In my mind I said, *Hector, you'll never catch me in your bed. I have a king-sized bed of my own that three of us can have a threesome.*

So when Hector looked at me, and both of us smiled at each other as we cleared the dinner table, I came to a place in my psyche that he is not only studying his wife's infidelity—even though his suspicion was just a suspicion without proof—but he is also studying if I'm one of his wife's lovers.

Zelda's misdirected sex text to Gordon that

went to him by mistake, and my saying that I don't know Gordon made him think I am covering for his wife; therefore, I am with his wife. Once in our trash talk about women who walked by on Flatbush and Church Avenues, he called me an "incorrigible ladies' man." I couldn't see the reason why he described me so. Both of us were admiring the women walking by; those women were our eye food especially women with great, big bottoms.

I immediately wanted to stop calling his wife Zee and call her Mrs. Hedgpine. But I felt by doing so I would let Hector know that I, too, was studying him, not as a buddy, but as a rival who would hurt me if he is certain that I had sex with his wife.

I knew his temper. I also knew Zelda's determination of taking risks. To her, a risk was like electricity and a negative and a positive pole will attract. But though that attraction was lethal, she went for it. Risk was in her DNA.

The phone rang early one morning, and I answered. "Hi, Zee. How is married life?"

"Hector is promoted at Homeland. He begged me for the description of the man who was reading in the subway car how to make a bomb, and I told him when he beseeched me day and night to tell him. He also said he wants to attend Elder T's lecture to know more about when he will be launching the UPI Flag."

"When is he coming home?"

"He did not tell me."

"How many friends you have on *Facebook* now? A friend told me that I have to be careful when writing to someone on *Facebook* because if I don't know the difference between *Message, Share, Comment,* and *Post,* my message may go not where I intended it to go."

"Why not say your uppity Haitian woman who calls President Jean-Bertrand Aristide 'a *Lavalas,*' meaning he is low class. Don't forget in April, 2003, Aristide declared Voodoo an officially recognized religion. He is a man for his people.

"Mulatto people with money in Haiti can no longer take little girls called '*Restavec*' to work long hours without paying them since President Aristide came in power. Elder T's UPI Flag should fly alongside Haiti's National Flag for the *Restavecs* who came out of bondage. They were kept in bondage by Haiti's uppities."

I was shocked by Zelda's knowledge of geo-politics. Then I remember that she came from Venezuela, a place that had many revolutions. Those revolutions were always supported by the downtrodden. I was glad to get away from her politics.

"Zee, how many friends you have on *Facebook* since your marriage?"

"Over ten thousand. My English is getting better because I have conversations in English with plenty people. I only spoke to twelve people in Spanish, and one of them knew my background. I stopped talking to her because she's too nosy."

"Is Zorro Zorro still sex texting you?"

"Yes."

"Don't forget you are married."

"And I have another friend with a nice *Facebook* name."

"What's his name?"

"Another One."

"C'mon."

"True."

"How true?"

"As the sun will come out tomorrow."

"The sky looks cloudy and gray to me, Zee. Were you here when the Texan weatherman said to women on live TV 'If rape is inevitable, lay back and enjoy it?'"

"I was a baby when the fool said that. But in my

research I learned he was fired as the words came out of his stupid mouth."

"Who else writes you?"

"Another One writes lovely *Facebook* letters."

"Did he send his résumé or some sort of biography?"

"I told him my name is May May Maryland."

"It couldn't be more alliterative. You described to your Homeland Security husband the man who was reading how to make bombs. I hope the day never comes that you will have to describe your *Facebook* character named Another One."

She smiled.

"Have you made a date with Another One ?"

"Yes; because you are hiding from me, and Hector is always away."

"Don't forget you talk in your sleep, and you tell the truth when your husband puts you to sleep after his Viagra's performance."

We laughed.

"Let's hope Another One and May May Maryland never become a true story. Don't forget everything in the waste basket of the computer can be retrieved. Homeland people know how to do that."

"I have nothing to hide, Stude Bakka."

"I hope so." I hung up.

5

I cooked a sumptuous dinner, and I was as happy with the taste on my palate as *CNN's* Anthony Bourdain was happy when eating chicken heads and drinking wine in Myanmar.

It was 10.07 p.m., and James Hood was playing *A God Lavender on Soundscapes* on Music Choice on Channel 892. I suffer from insomnia but refused to go back on *Ambien*. I called Zelda and told her I saw a better name for her *Facebook* friend instead of Zorro Zorro.

"What is it, Stude?"

"God Lavender."

"I am a good Catholic. I don't make joke with God's name."

"Zee, I recommend that name because if you happen to wrongly direct your text to Mr. Homeland, using the name God Lavender, he'll think your elevator doesn't go upstairs."

"With his Homeland Security mind, he'll think

that's not Catholic communion wine, and he will check the water in the tap."

"And if he does that, what you'd tell him?"

"I'll say, honey, is something wrong?"

"And you'll drink the water and call it city champagne to make him comfortable?"

"I will pour out a glass to see if he'll drink it."

"So you have your way of testing whether he'd trust you."

"Not every time, but sometimes. Hold on, Stude. Hector is calling…Honey, Stude and I are talking about you."

"About what?"

"About how trusting you are with me. When are you coming home, my love?"

"Click."

"Stude, are you still holding on?"

"Yes. How is Hector?"

"We got cut off, and I think it was deliberate."

"Why do you think so, Zee?"

"My psyche tells me when I will die."

"So you will die the next time he cuts you off the phone?"

"I don't want to discuss it. Goodnight."

I was groggy with sleep. Tom Barabas was play-

ing *Riding the Rainbow*, one of his romantic rhap-
sodies, and I was thinking of a sad day when Hector and I may need healing rain to prevent us from
hating each other because of Zelda's guile. But then I
told myself that I will always abide by what my sage,
Dr. Eli Balboza, sociologist extraordinaire, said to me
alone. "You and Hector are two blind fools craving
Zelda's love, and her love is on a pole that is a moving
target. She is like Lucy who never let Charlie Brown
kick the football."

"Dr. Eli, I'm not in love with her."

"Stude, you are such a liar. The way you described her to me…" She never ended the sentence.

The first time that I saw Dr. Eli, I was running
through the winding halls of Medgar Evers College to
go to the cafeteria. Coming abreast of her, my left eye
glanced at her right side. I saw a hanging strand of her
curly hair; and I said to myself, in Trinidad and Tobago's dub prose, "Ah sure she's ah *Dougla* (bi-racial)
ooman."

Then I remember a *Dougla* girl jilted me and
broke my heart when I was nineteen years old. I
vowed never to love a *Dougla* woman again. My lips
said that, not my heart.

Whom Balboza jilted before coming to Medgar Evers came to mind, but I quickly dropped that thought. Then I said to myself, that Balboza woman is too decent to break anyone's heart. She's probably a professor.

On that very day that I saw Dr. Balboza, I was beaming over my 4.0 Grade Point Average that semester. I wanted to share my joy of a perfect score with her. But I didn't, because she was a stranger to me.

On investigation I learned she taught Sociology at Medgar; and one day I strayed into her class to know if she were as good in Sociology as Professor Monroe Goutier, my English teacher, was good in English. I matched them on even keel.

She is a Senior Research Fellow at the Caribbean Research Center, Professor of Social and Behavioral Sciences, an archivist and researcher in carnival traditions.

Later in our friendship, and after her overt examination of me, and found there was no blemish on my character, she made me a Trustee on her Trinidad and Tobago Carnival Board. She was easy to address; she cared about my welfare; and she was nonjudgmental.

Hence, she had my confidence, and my eyes were on her beauty without sexuality in mind or in thought. She is my Gamaliel, a teacher of Saul of Tarsus, and I bow to her for knowledge from the day I have known her.

Now it was easy for me to introduce my buddy, Hector, to her. Without a second thought, we brought her into our lives and we asked her what to expect from a woman with guile. Smart like the fox, Dr. Eli said, "Stude and Hector, why do you think I will know what all women think?"

"Just asking," Hector said.

"Stude?"

"Just asking."

"Well, I don't."

Dr. Balboza showed sociology and psychology in her smile and tested our knowledge of how sociology is commonsense. She said, "Gentlemen, a primary group shares-human intimacies. Now, if a Delta Airline is filled with carnival-celebrant strangers traveling from New York to go to Florida to celebrate Miami carnival, what would make them become a group: Those who love the Catholic God; those who love the Anglican God; or those who are members of ISIS murderous gang from Syria on board the plane? What is your answer, Hector?"

"I am a casual Catholic, so I will say those who

love the Catholic God."

"Stude?"

"I don't believe in any special god. But since Hector picked those who believe in the Catholic God, I will pick those who believe in the Anglican God."

"Think, gentlemen. Both your Gods are the same."

Neither of us answered.

Dr. Balboza looked at us as two dummies without commonsense, as she spoke. "The ISIS murderous gang from Syria on the plane will make those strangers, who believe in their gods, become a *group* because they will join as one, and think of ways to save their lives. Those strangers will get together, irrespective of the gods they serve, and they will think with one head of how they can kill those ISIS kidnappers. That is sociology, a testament to know if what we see is reality or not.

"Of the behavioral sciences, I love teaching sociology, and I come alive when my students, especially the millennials—18 to 30—test my knowledge with their pop questions to see if I'm hip and up to date with hip-hop trends. My answer to them is, 'Remember nothing is new under the sun. One thing I have, for sure, above every one of you is that I was born before you. I know what you are now learning, and you don't know what I forgot."

Hector and I saw the wisdom in the Professor's answer, and we were ready to pour out what we feared about a woman's scorn, a woman's guile, and a woman's revenge. We believed her answer wouldn't be women versus men, but it would be what humans do for their conscience's sake or for their survival. Although Hector works as a sleuth in Homeland Security, I became the spokesman to deliver our cases in third person to dear Dr. Balboza.

Hector said his only woman is Zelda, and Zelda is his world.

I told Dr. Eli that I had invited Iris, the woman I intended to marry, to spend a weekend with me. As she entered my house she said, "Stude, for the amount of years you have been living in America, you don't have a nicer house than this? I thought you were living in a better neighborhood. Get rid of those Puerto Rican curtains. I hate red curtains. All your furniture needs changing. Move out those dinosaurs that live in your kitchen before I move in."

I told her they are keepsakes.

She said, "I only sleep on designers' sheets from Macy's."

I told her that I couldn't afford them. I had in mind to prepare a fine dinner for us, but I was disgusted with her presence. I ordered Chinese take-out, and told her to leave. She was happy to leave me with my dinosaurs; and I was over-joyed when she left.

"Why didn't you take down the Puerto Rican curtains and promise that you will buy Macy's designer's sheets to see if she will sleep over and give you the goodies?" Dr. Eli asked, and laughed aloud.

"Hell, no!"

One day I ate my pride and phoned her. A man's voice answered. I put down the phone and never called her again. But I was glad for the next caller who didn't give me time to speak.

"Stude Bakka, why don't you call me? You stopped having lunch with me. I hardly hear from Hector, and now I have forty thousand friends on *Facebook*. *Facebook* is a modern phenomenon, and I will use it to advertise my play. I am going to write a play for the world to read. It will be called PEEPING THROUGH THE KEYHOLE, SHE LEARNED ABOUT LIFE, ABOUT LOVE, AND ABOUT SEX. Can you come over now to read my first draft?"

"Sure. I'm in your neighborhood." As I walked in her beautiful apartment, I said, "Zee, is your play going to be a story of individualism and community?"

"No. It will be a story of conflict, of origins, of insight, of gender, and of identity."

In my mind I said, *when and where the fuck this Venezuelan woman got all this knowledge of 'literature across cultures.' When she came to this country, she used a noun and a verb to make a sentence, and I had to decipher what she meant. The man who is teaching her English is either a genius or she was fucking with my and Hector's brains telling us she doesn't know English.*

"Zee, give me a synopsis of your play."

"It will be based on a precocious, little girl peeping through a keyhole in her parent's house, and she learns about sex; and when that little girl becomes a woman and falls in love with loveless sex, she sends a sex text to her lover, and by mistake the sex text went to her husband. How it sounds, Stude, my best friend who never tries to get me in bed because he's afraid Hector will blow his brain with his revolver?"

"Zee, Hector and I know that's your bio written in third person. We know all the acts in that play." I sat on the loveseat.

"Does your sociologist broad know all the acts in my play, too?"

"If you are referring to Dr. Balboza, she is a lady."

"Is she pretty?"

"Why do you want to know that?"

"Prettier than me?" She took off her top, and pulled off her slacks. "Look at me, Stude. She's not a broad like me, but you told me she's half-breed like me."

"I can't remember telling you that."

"Did she ever try to teach you the sociology of wayward sex? And how satisfying it is when lovers have make-up sex?"

"I sit in her class for knowledge *only*."

She walked away. "I'm going to make a private call to check Hector's whereabouts." She came back in a diaphanous gown with nothing below.

"Are you about to go to bed?"

"With you."

"I thought you invited me to edit the first draft of your play." I read the play, and I shook with fear of what may happen to her or to Hector in the future.

"We can multitask. We can read the draft, and test your strength on me."

As a single man, I have lived a life of debauchery, and women never had to ask me to test my manhood. My mind roamed, and I hated my cowardice because I was afraid to even look at the naked body lying on the love seat in front of me.

First, I looked at her silky afro beautifully coifed. Then I compared her breasts with others that I've touched, slept on, nibbled on, bit on, cried on, and I'm still searching to see if any is as beautiful as Zelda's with hard, ripened nipples.

I've looked at women's breasts in books of erotica; I've studied Elder Thébaud's paintings of African virgins' breasts, and my body came warm with affection. I've turned, slowly, every page of Uwe Ommer South African *Black Ladies*, with breasts of every size, some barely covered with sea sand and the evening rays of the sun on them. But I've never seen breasts as beautiful as Zelda Hedgpine's.

They were God's creation for her only. They were the size of grapefruits, less swarthy than the color of her face, and her swarthier nipples pointed sinfully at me. If Adam had seen Zelda's breasts, he would never have had lust for Eve's. Thus, he never would have sinned, and the world would be void of sinners like me.

I am Stude Bakka, the son of Mary Bakka, and a sinner from birth. The colonial rulers in Trinidad and Tobago had my name written on my birth certificate "Illegitimate Boy" because my father did not marry my mother. My mind continued to roam from the past to the present and *vice versa* to get my thoughts away from what was before me.

The phone rang; and she put it on speaker. "Zelda, I heard you left a message for me. What do you want?"

"Honey, I bet you can never guess what I'm doing? You want me to tell you what?"

Oh my god! I hope she isn't speaking to Hector. She looked at me and began playing with her nipples as if they were drinking straws. I hadn't prayed to God in many years so an *ad hoc* prayer to Him to prevent Zelda from putting her breasts in my face may not be granted by Him.

In times like these one must have a savior, so I went to a time in my life that gave me rage, not for sex, but for letting a woman know that I am a man, and I need respect. I resurrected a long past incident with my boss, and invoked my rage and anger against my boss to prevent me from breaking my promise to Hector that I will never cohabit with his wife.

That long past incident was with my cocky boss named Naomi Zidd. She was a new graduate lawyer from an Ivy League university. I was her first secretary. She had called me in for dictation, and I knew I could transcribe her deposition from shorthand to English in half an hour. As I came out of her office, I went and typed an idea for my book, *Grenada Ghost*. Ideas came flooding, and flooding, and flooding. And I kept typing those new ideas for my new book instead of transcribing my shorthand notes to English for Naomi Zidd's deposition.

She buzzed me. "Stude, where is my work?"

"I'm typing it, Ms. Zidd."

"I'm in a hurry. My client and I will be having lunch, and I need a draft to show him."

I knew she was pissed, but I had to meet a deadline for publication of my book. "Give me five minutes more."

"I want it now." She rushed outside.

"Give me two minutes more, Ms. Zidd."

"What were you typing before?"

I did not answer.

"Stude, what were you typing all the time?"

"Give me one minute, Ms. Zidd."

"I'm going to show you that you were typing your personal work and not my deposition." She pushed me away from the typewriter, pulled out my drawer, and showed me what I was typing. "You are a liar."

It was the first time I realize how simple can a man commit murder. I did not murder Naomi with a dagger. But I did so with my nasty tongue. I cursed her so loud that the full staff—lawyers, partners, clerks, messengers, stenographers, and paralegals—on the twenty eighth floor of the tallest building on Water Street, New York, New York, were our audience. I grabbed the manuscript of my book from her hand, picked up my bag, and attempted to walk out because I knew, for sure, I will be fired.

Naomi pulled me into her office, slammed the door, and hugged me. She was crying. "Stude, as a child, my father has never gone into my drawers; as a busy teenager, my father has never spied on me or gone into my drawers to see if I had condoms or birth control pills; and here I am sniping your manhood." Her tears were soaking my shirt. "Please, Stude, I want you to go back and finish transcribing my work. And I want you to forgive me."

I started crying. "Naomi, I want you to forgive me, too."

We were like two crying children.

"Sit down, Stude." Both of us sat.

We looked at each other as brother and sister who just had a fight over trifles, but made up in love when we heard our grumpy father's footsteps.

"What did you say about my lipstick, Stude?" She stifled her laugher.

"I'm not listening to you. I have my boss's work to do."

Both of us could never control our laughter whenever we meet in an empty elevator.

As I overcame thinking of that past incident with Naomi Zidd, Zelda pushed me down on the loveseat, and screamed. She had told me before that her screams were similar to her mother's. As a teenager that's the scream she heard when she peeped through the keyhole. Her screams were erotic. The way she romanced herself and looked lovingly at me, intuited what parts of her body turn her on most, and I should touch those parts. I could see she was ready to go, and she wanted a man's gristle deep in her.

I could feel nitric oxide by my genitals, and I was turned on. My brain, my most sensitive sexual organ, was speaking silently to me, then noisily. From childhood, all my mischiefs took place in my brain; and in manhood all my sins take place in my brain, too. Somehow, my brain was telling me to refrain from ripping Zelda's thong. There wasn't much to rip. It was a string shaped in a triangle.

I was hearing the forethought and judgment of my frontal lobes arousing my penis. I never thought she was beautiful. I only thought she was attractive. But as I looked into her brown eyes, looked at her naked body for a long time, I realize she was both attractive and beautiful. I thought of Hector's friendship, and my nerve cells woke me up. I stared at her body until my eyes became red; and I imagined Hector's footsteps walking in on us.

"Why won't you do it, Stude. My mother loves men, and I have her genes. Yesterday I went to confession, and I told Father in the confession box of how I feel when I want sex, and he told me, 'Go and pray, my child.' When I peeped through the keyhole I liked what the Dictator did to my mother. If I tell you, you'll do it to me? Please answer."

I did not answer.

"I am my mother's only child, and she trusted me. She told me my father has erectile dysfunction, and he gave her permission to have sex with the Dictator and any man she wants to, but she must do it only in the house, and never go to a hotel.

"I called Hector's job, and I was told he is on an

assignment in Pakistan. Stude, please, fuck me. So many men want to fuck me. Why won't you?"

"I think I got a dose of STD."

"You are lying. You want to maintain your honor for Hector's sake. Neither love nor honor is a criterion to me."

She embraced me as if we were nudists on the beach in the Dominican Republic. "I can see you are uncomfortable with my nakedness, so lift me to the bedroom to find clothes, and then I'll play a song for you on the keyboard."

My hands touched her full body as I lifted her up. Her body was soft as silk. And I did not sin. "What are you going to play, Zee?"

"I'm going to play *The Lies of Handsome Men* because I know you like to hear when Sara Gazarek sings it. When I went inside I saw a text on my cell from Hector saying he'll be here soon, so let me prepare lunch for three of us. Would you stay for lunch?"

After she played *The Lies of Handsome Men* on the keyboard, she put on a CD with Andy Bey singing *Speak Low*. She put out her hand, and I danced with her.

My heart was beating from fear, and mind was saying, "This fucking woman is crazy! She practices tragedies as often as I practice showering without soap when I forget to buy." And before I collected my senses on how I could have been killed by my best friend who suspects I am humping his wife, I heard the echo of my voice. "Zee, I'm hearing my voice. Where is it coming from?"

"I taped our love affair on my cell, Stude Bakka."

"What! What! What! You are a fucking crazy woman!"

"I'm crazy in love with you. And I'll never forget you. The Thursday night that you took me in I had nowhere to go and sleep. On the Wednesday I slept by a man. He lives on the East Side, and from his loft I could see the boats on the East River. He boasted about his Fortune-500 company."

"Is he a brother with plenty of that green stuff you find in the Treasury?"

"No. He is Waspy. We made love the whole night. In the morning he made breakfast. We showered together. We dressed together. He fondled me while we were dressing. He said he has to make a phone call and to wait for him by the conductor car in the subway.

"I waited by the conductor car. He came. He

looked me in the eye. He passed me without saying a word, and when I went to sit on the empty seat next to him, he got up, moved without talking to me, and sat next to a white woman who lives in his building.

"The beating that my first husband gave to me is less hurtful than the way that man snubbed me. His racism hurts, and it hurts more because he used my body and gave me money as a 'mess of pottage.'"

I did not know what to say to ease her pain of racism knowing her father was white. The words I found were, "There are better days to come, Zee. God is watching the just and the unjust." And her sadness showed her beauty.

"You ever saw him again?"

"No. He called me many times, and I did not answer. He sent large checks to my mailbox, and I destroyed them."

She started to cry and say that I am her best friend who took her in with no strings attached. I hugged her tenderly, and told her when I came to New York for the first time I landed at Kennedy Airport on a cold night without a coat, not knowing where to go because the person who promised to pick me up and accommodate me until I get a place of my own, reneged on her promise. But a stranger took me in.

I kissed her on her cheek and left for home thinking of all the immigrants who came to this country and endured hardships and are still suffering hardships. Some who have climbed above their hardships, and are reaping the largesse of this land; and those with "derailed dreams," who are still struggling. They are still searching to see the light at the end of the tunnel, to become citizens of this great land called America.

6

Two years had passed, and I heard nothing from Zelda or Hector. Dr. Eli Balboza, carnival archivist, reconfirmed my appointment as Trustee on the New York Carnival Board. She invited many scholars from Trinidad and Tobago to speak on the impact of carnival on the businesses, on the masqueraders, and why only the merchants get the plums and profits from Trinidad and Tobago's carnival.

The meeting was held at the United Nations, and it was chaired by Dr. Balboza. Apart from the interesting topics on carnival that were discussed at length, I learned a lot of the new kind of sociological thinking of a majority of the people in Trinidad and Tobago from one of the speakers on the forum in our side bar. I gathered from him that the natives from Trinidad and Tobago who live abroad are "treated as expatriates," when they return to the country of their birth.

Being called an "expatriate" and "treated as an

expatriate" was no shock to me. I had gone home to Fyzabad, after eight years away, and I had corrected my younger sister, Julie, on a mistake she had made about a private family matter.

She said, "Stude, not because you are living in America you know more than me. All you people who leave here and go to England, especially those who went to America, think they are better than we down here."

As a naturalized citizen of America, I learn and practice the American culture and lingo: "If you can't beat 'em, join 'em."

I instituted a new kind of discourse with Julie. I reverted to speaking of my life as a farm boy when I went to the fields to plant rice, corn, and other ground provisions for sale. I remained on down-home talks, and there were no quarrels or hard feelings with the folks in our parents' house.

When I was dressed to return Brooklyn, Julie kissed me. She was satisfied with my farm-boy behavior, and said, "Stude, you haven't changed a bit. You are the same thing as when you lived down here. You are not as some of those fools who come down from America and showoff talking about climate science."

Having left the meeting at the United Nations,

I was still thinking of Dr. Balboza's wide knowledge of all that pertains to Trinidad and Tobago carnival. As I stepped inside my house, the telephone rang; I snatched it; and the caller said, "Wrong number."

Somehow my mind ran on the way Zelda was treated in the subway by *that* man after he had pleasured his body with hers and then pretended he doesn't know her when he was among his kith and kin. I had tried to find Zelda and Hector many times, but to no avail. Nonetheless, I never changed my address, my phone number, or the lock to my apartment. I felt one day they will walk back into my life. Then an e-mail walked into my life as I turned my computer on:

Stude Bakka, this is Zee. How are you, my best friend? How is your séance adviser, Dr. Balboza? (Smile). You are as scarce as hen's teeth. Did Hector call you to let you know that we are no longer husband and wife? Our parting was painful.

You were there when we were married in Divine Truth Assembly, and I told Pastor Enid Bain that I will personally take the documents we signed in church to the City Registrar. Pastor Bain said it was her responsibility to mail those documents to the City Registrar, but I told her I will be in the neighborhood and will hand deliver the documents to the City Reg-

istrar Office. She looked at me, quizzically, but finally gave me the documents to deliver by hand.

Pastor Bain took back the documents in the large envelope, and I wanted to know why. Then she prayed over the envelope and gave it back to me and said, "Walk with God in all of your dealings." I told Pastor Bain, "I always walk with God, and I will hand deliver the marriage documents we signed in church to be officially registered for the Government's archives."

Stude, I did not mail or hand deliver the documents to register and make legal my and Hector's marriage. So we were never married, and Hector does not know this. He had given me a rock diamond. Ask Dr. Balboza, that woman you always boast about as if she's doctor-know-it-all, if I should return the ring.

Hector and I went our different ways. I don't know where he is, and he doesn't know where I am, but he promised that he will kill me when he finds me. I know he can find me. He is a Homeland Security investigator, but I am not afraid to die because my life is trash in New York.

I will repeat what I've told you before: This is not the life I expected to live when I came to America. In Caracas I drove in a limousine with an official plate. I ate the best meals. I had money from the Dictator, not pocket change, but plenty money. I helped poor people in the barrios. They called me Baby Santa.

Hector and I separated because of a misdirected letter that went to him, but it was for my Zorro Zorro, my man with azure eyes. I tried to kill my feelings for Zorro Zorro because I still love Hector but my love for Hector is just brotherly. I had to write Zorro Zorro to ease the excessive, sexual tension within me. Here is the text I wrote:

Zorro Zorro, when I looked into your eyes the last time we met, my clitoris went on fire. I want to fetishize eroticism as if you are the Spanish bull chasing me, and I am waiting for you to gore my inside again.

Zorro Zorro, I keep dreaming of you every night, and the nights do come in clusters when I burn for you. I enjoyed everything that that night made real. Even your whipping when you tied me to the bedpost, though not a new experience because David did it with a real whip and with real blows. But I enjoyed your playful whipping and your knee bending to find my thick turf. You are probably wondering if the words I use are from my brain. No. I used a Spanish dictionary, an English dictionary, A Grammar Book for Dummies, and Elements of Style.

I made sure that I always use an objective pronoun after a preposition, and a nominative pronoun after the verb to be. *My private teacher—I won't tell you his name—stressed that grammar rule because he hates hearing so many TV Announcers, Talk-Show hosts and Politicians flout the rules of syntax.*

Hector doesn't know I have a private English teacher. We are even because he never told me that his dog, Betsy, came first in his life; but that was easy to tell. I hope you can tell that you are first in my life.

Zorro Zorro, my love, every muscle in my body answered to your deep kisses that dragged my tonsils. I love you, my idol. Why? Every vein that you glided over with your rough tongue hardened the teats of my breasts; and when you surfed to my bushy field and lingered before penetration, I cried with ecstasy.

I don't know why my Venezuelan blood needs your Spanish blood but whenever we meet, my knees buckle especially after we drink that nameless wine in those unmarked bottles and we smoke that stuff. Once I asked you why is this happening to me, and your answer was: "My love for you, May May, is always freshly ground with the spices of the god of love." My love for you, Zorro Zorro, is tasty like the water dripping out of the cured earth and tasty like the water in the oasis that quenches thirsty souls. Only you have drunk deep in my black-and-white well.

Zorro Zorro, no man ever made me feel the way you do, and I, a nymph, by design, have had many men. I will put my neck under the Englishman's guillotine to save you. I will do that for no one else. Social media brought me to you. First, it was Facebook, then texting. They brought my body and soul to you. I never touch POST that all eyes can read what I say to you. I touch your visage on Facebook and that touch makes it possible that only you can read what I write.

Hector thinks he can decode my password because he works at Homeland Security and has all the tools there to decode terrorists' texts, so he thinks my password is easy to decode. I was the friend of a Dictator for nineteen years, and he taught me lots of things that I wouldn't say to a soul.

Hector will never know that I write calligraphy with saliva on your hairy chest when your body is over me. I turn the ways you like to view my tattoos; I love the way you chew on them and groan when I pull you down to eat me on my aching back. Your perspiration bathes me with joy.

Many nights I pray to Mary to forgive me because I love you more than my decent husband, but his true love burdens me. I am afraid of the way he loves me. *When his sex is weak, he becomes violent. He smashes dishes. He turns over tables; he threatens me; but he never hits me.*

Meet me at our rendezvous, Zorro Zorro, my prince. Treat me as the pauper. Bring no prickly roses or black Godiva chocolates. My nipples and my vagina must be the only black pieces lying in bed tomorrow.

I've just finished reading HEROTICA, A Collection of Women's Erotica Fiction, edited by Susie Bright, and I will do to you what some of those lovers do to their men and women. ZH

I phoned Dr. Balboza and read the sex text from Zelda Hedgpine. "What do you think, Dr. Eli?"

"Stude Bakka, that Venezuelan nymphomaniac is fucking with you and Hector's head." The word fucking came out of her mouth and sounded as the Pope's Imprimatur to unholy Catholics. I pretended I did not hear her. I wanted to hear her pronunciation of the predicate fucking one more time.

"What did you say, Dr. Eli?"

"She's fucking up your heads, you two fools! Too many times she misdirected her bullshit texts. Can't you see it is a game she's playing for Hector to swallow her line, hook, and sinker, and for him to get turned on and do what the Dictator did to her mother? She wanted the gristle, but not in the Christian pose. She has an ax to grind. She wants him to have public sex with somebody peeping through the keyhole.

"I am correcting Sociology 101 test papers. The students are using your books, *Ice and Eyes in the Sun* and *Grenada Ghost* this term; and they like both. The women say you were a naughty boy when you were young and carefree, and they hated you at the beginning of *Ice and Eyes in the Sun*; but they see your humanity at the ending of your true story. The students were shocked when they found out who is the murderer in *Grenada Ghost*. I'll see you soon."

"How soon? I do not trust Hector's mood these days."

"Wait on my call. Tell Hector that I'll be there soon."

"The truth is: I haven't seen Hector for two years or more."

"But you just said you can't trust his mood."

"That was just an instinctive thought, and most times my instinct is right."

"Whether your instinctive thought is right or wrong, you'll see me soon."

I, too, felt Zelda purposely misdirected her sex texts to Hector. Why? She's no novice on her ambient devices. She is as good on the computer as King LeBron James on Cleveland Basketball Team is good in dunking sky balls into the hoop. But why she left Hector? I called Zelda's cell number, and a man's voice said, "I don't know who is Zee."

"I emphasized the words Zelda Hedgpine."

He slammed the phone down.

Instantly, I had a worried mind. Why did Hector and Zee, the two love-hate birds, split? Did he find her and Zorro Zorro in bed? Zee is too smart to bring a man in Hector's bed knowing that her first husband beat her as if he were beating a snake just for suspecting a man was in her bed; and her present man works for Homeland Security and hid his gun from her. I remember what his father did to his mother.

I wanted to travel to their old address, but I changed my mind. I thought I would not get back on time for my book reading at the United Peoples Inclusive Center, run by Elder T. The book reading was well attended. Elder T's books, *Pearls of Inspiration* and *Global Caribbean Representation—By Our Peoples' Will—from Grassroots Up* were sold out.

Elder T reminded the vast audience about the

hoisting of the UPI Flag in May 2016. A man shouted, "Elder T, I am of East Indian descent. I come from the Republic of Trinidad and Tobago, and my East Indian parents have many flags in different colors on bamboo poles in their back yard. What is the difference with my parents' flags from your UPI flag? And how could you be launching a flag on American soil? America already has her national flag."

"Sir, what is your name?" Elder T asked.

"Ali."

"Ali, the proper approach to answering your question calls, first, for rectifying your misperceptions of facts regarding the United Peoples Flag. Though its name vividly depicts intent and purpose as a rallying emblem of unity within the human species, its unique approach towards global harmony obviously challenges our standard thought process. Ali, this Global Peoples Flag Hoisting fosters mutual recognition and respect as the precursor to reconcile our adversity rather than using our unique gifts to foster disunity. Ali, if I'm going too fast for you, let me know."

"Don't you think I have sense to understand your diatribe?"

Elder T smiled. "I know you have sense, Ali. But, in the first portion of your three-part question, it is perceived that global hoisting of the United Peoples Flag marginalizes others based on national, cultural, and religious diversity. This is a material misinterpretation of the United Peoples Flag's global hoisting. This enactment aims to celebrate the infinite array of virtues embodied by the human species. Are you there with me, Ali?" Elder T looked at his audience at 1601 Nostrand Avenue, Brooklyn, and when he saw Ali's shining forehead, he got a new kind of vigor to speak.

"Ali, the second part of your question seems to emphasize that *different* means *separate*. Yes! The Peoples Flag to be hoisted is different from your parents' which is sectarian. UPI's bridges cultural diversities involving all peoples recognizing that it is the sum total of all parts that complete the whole.

"Ali, let me end by saying that the last part of your question should note that the United Peoples Flag does not compete with any national or traditional flag. This flag symbolizes the embodiment of our entire human species, and, thus, no individual, group, or nation, can justifiably proclaim ownership of the United Peoples Flag."

"Elder T, are you a constitutional lawyer?"

"I am no kind of lawyer. Are you?"

"Yes. And you are threading on a constitutional matter way above your head."

"Ali, do you know that basic needs of oppressed peoples would be amply met as we get to know each other, you included, from grass-root up. It's an innate virtue to be activated. We the Peoples must come to the rescue. By the way, Ali, what Constitution you are talking about?"

Before Ali had time to answer, a member of Elder T's flock recited the Mission Statement of United Peoples Inclusive and other members followed: *We come together just a few, to give ourselves wisely, that all may receive sufficiently.*

"That is our covenant to each of us—you, too, Ali."

The meeting ended but Ali's voice echoed on Nostrand Avenue: "You are a charlatan! You are a charlatan! You are a charlatan."

Elder T, six feet, two, a handsome man, smiled at Ali's rant and rave, and said softly to the members of UPI, Inc., "See what I've been telling you of people who boast of knowing the Constitution, but don't have functional education."

Being a Caribbean man, of all the seasons, I love summer best. In summer I navigate on foot like a hungry ant searching for food. I find transport on the subway, on the ferry boats, on the Circle Line, and in friends' vehicles that take me throughout the five boroughs of New York and to our neighbor, New Jersey, the Garden State. Every morning I pick a yellow rose from my flower garden and give that rose to the first woman I meet on my way to the subway. Summer always puts me in a romantic mood.

The traveling jitters hit me, and I left Brooklyn and went to Princeton, New Jersey, to buy a Princeton sweat shirt for my grandson, Caleb Gibson. I went to buy that sweat shirt with the hope that he will like it, and when he graduates from Hunter College he will go to Princeton University. I have a love for Princeton University after my friend, Joanna Elizabeth Haye, gave me a tour of that university when she was a freshman there.

When I went to Princeton University and heard Dr. Alison Gammie introduce Joanna Elizabeth Haye to the audience before Haye defended her dissertation for her Ph.D. on Defense on 'Dynamics of the Mismatch Repair Complexes during DNA Replication,' I was blown away by Haye's scientific knowledge and articulation.

My computer went bad again, and I had no

intention of buying another. Suddenly, I wanted a computer so that I could email Dr. Haye's discussions to my granddaughter, Ashaki, who is on a one-year scholarship at Einstein's School of Medicine in New York.

I knew Haye at the age of seventeen. And to hear her imparting such knowledge made me feel ignorant of everything there is to know.

After I bought the sweat shirt, I walked the streets as a lost child; I sat on a bench on Nassau Street a hand length away from an electric pole covered with flyers. Myriads of flyers advertising how to end belly pain, and where to go to buy a pot to piss in if you are over three hundred pounds never drew my attention.

What drew my full attention was when a young woman in rumpled clothes as if she just got up from sleeping in the grass pulled the flyer that was hanging and repeated the words on that flyer to her friend just as shabbily rumpled: "PEEPING THROUGH THE KEYHOLE, SHE LEARNED ABOUT LIFE, ABOUT LOVE, AND ABOUT SEX, based on a true story will be in Princeton University...."

I thought I was dreaming but I got to my senses when the couple reached the corner of Nassau Street and Park Place. I ran down Nassau Street, jumped over the barricade that blocked the repaired section on Nassau Street, and while I was running I heard a man say, "The city is always fixing the fucking street this week, and digging up the same fucking spot next week."

But before the disheveled-looking couple turned into Park Place, I shouted, "Sir! Sir! Miss! Miss! Wait, please."

They looked at me.

"Yes! Yes! You! You! Please, wait."

They waited.

"Can I, please, read the strip of paper you took off the electric pole?"

"Sure." They handed me the flyer.

I looked at the flyer. It was damp and words were missing. "Can you tell me if that is still taking place at Princeton University?"

"It ended last week. I took the strip for my scrap book," the young woman said.

"Where was it held?"

"At the university in Lewis Thomas 003 Hall."

'For how long?"

"We really don't know." They answered as a chorus. "But it was a great play."

"Do you know any of the actors?"

"No," they said in unison.

"What can you tell me about the play?"

"A woman texted a letter to her lover; she touched the wrong *send* button; and the text went to her husband by mistake."

"Miss, Sir, I will give you fifty dollars if you answer three questions. Hold this bill. It could be yours."

The young woman looked at her equally young companion and said, "Okay. What are the questions?"

"Did you see the play?"

The female spoke. "Yes. But I slept halfway through it because I was tired from studying for finals. Ask him. Both of us were there."

"Young man, you and your friend are very polite and trusting."

"That's how we are in Princeton."

"Where do you go to school?"

"At Princeton U."

"Wow! My first question is: Who are the characters in the play?"

"Zorro Zorro, May May, and I can't remember the static actors' names."

"What else?"

"There was a distraction, to me, a definite distraction."

"What do you mean?"

"I do not know if it is real or part of the play, but a man brandished his gun and left before the guards could get hold of him."

"How come he got away?"

"Mister, here is your money," the young woman said. "You are asking us detective questions because we pulled off a flyer from an electric pole."

"No more questions, Miss. Keep the money. I thank you and your friend very much."

I could hear the young woman talking under her breath: "That fucking creep! I wish I could get some of what he's smoking."

I invented a studio smile when I saw a well-dressed woman walking up Nassau Street. In that university town people are casually dressed. And, to me, that woman looked as a misfit. "Madam, how are you? Could you, please, tell me where I could get a taxi to take me to the train at Princeton Junction?"

She took out her phone and touched knobs. "You have a pen? Write. Call 609-924-7300, and ask for Randy. He is as reliable as they come."

"Thank you very much."

As I rode back to New York, I had a plan. And that plan was to get to Brooklyn and go back on *Face-*

book. I knew my friend, Dr. Joanna Elizabeth Haye, was on *Facebook*. As I opened my door and kicked off my hot and sweaty sneakers, I went to my computer.

On *Facebook,* I wrote: "Dr. Jo, do you remember when I was at Princeton University to hear your Ph.D. Defense, and you, Georgia, Winston, Sammy, and I sat on a bench by an electric pole after you treated us to breakfast? That electric pole had thousands of flyers glued to it on Nassau Street.

"I sat on that same bench today (09/08/14), and I heard there was a play at your university called *PEEPING THROUGH THE KEYHOLE, SHE LEARNED ABOUT LIFE, ABOUT LOVE, AND ABOUT SEX.* It will be back at Princeton University. Since you live in Princeton, could you, please, tell me when next that play will be at Princeton U?"

"Stude, I am in South Dakota on my way to pick up a job as a postdoctoral researcher at the University of Southern California. My boyfriend, Vic, is driving me there; and I'm seeing some of the most beautiful scenery in America."

"Could you ask Dr. Gammie, your adviser, who still lectures at Princeton, when will the play be back at Princeton?"

Two days later I got a reply from Dr. Jo.

"I called Dr. Gammie. She is out of town, and she said she doesn't know."

"Call her again to ask one of her friends or fellow professors to find out when that play is coming back to the university."

I went and made a peanut-butter-jelly sandwich and drank two glasses of water. I hate water with a passion, but my urologist advised me strongly that I should drink more water "to prevent those kidney stones from coming back." When I came back from licking the jelly off my fingers, I saw writing on my computer from a distance.

"Stude, the play went overseas."

"Where, Dr. Jo?"

"Australia."

"For how long?"

"The people Dr. Gammie asked didn't know."

I searched on my computer to find the whereabouts of the play, but I really don't know how to find information on the computer as children in kindergarten do. Then I wondered if Hector really left his job at Homeland Security or if he was fired because of all his emotional quagmires—all the quagmires came about on account of his fathomless and jealous love for Zelda; and more so because he couldn't mold her the way he molded other women.

But then I thought could he be in Australia with the play. I wondered if he was the person who pointed a gun at the actors on stage hoping to kill Zorro Zorro or May May Maryland but the guards at Princeton did not hold him. I was also thinking if Zelda played herself as May May and Hector as Zorro Zorro.

I remembered Hector hates acting since a terrorist killed his dog, Betsy. Hector's overworked line is: "I am no actor. Probably I will play someone else when St. Peter stops me from entering heaven's pearly gate to look for Betsy. Only Betsy could make me believe there's life after death."

I became a Knot Zen: I was in a vision but even as a Zen I couldn't unravel my dreams of where the play is taking place. When is it leaving Australia, and where is it going after leaving Australia?

I was very tired. I went to bed repeating all those questions to myself, questioning myself and finding answers for my questions: Why not check the door to see if it is locked before I fall asleep and dream? Nobody comes in here except that friendly mouse that plays music on the keyboard when it is trying to get a nut stuck between the notes. I know the door is not locked, but I'm not getting up…Probably Zee will make a surprise visit, and I'll break my promise to Hector, and Zee and I will make love.

7

In my dream I relived the discussions on E. Wayne McDonald's two-day film show on events in the Caribbean and in Guyana; and I found myself smiling in my dream when the word *Culture* became a circular disagreement between Dr. Eli Balboza on the podium and Joseph Robinson in the audience. Neither, I assure you, had wine beforehand to lubricate the rapidity of their questions and answers that flowed effortlessly but with their passion.

Robinson, sporting a white goatee, had the audience laughing aloud, when he informed Caribbean people, who were the preponderance in the audience, of what should not be considered as *Culture*.

He pointed to the lone woman on the podium. "You call what those women do on Eastern Parkway on West Indian Labor Day Carnival *Culture*?" He emphasized the word *Culture* to drive home his point. "Those women who show that part of their body to the public that they should only show to their husbands and to their gynecologists, you call that display of showing their private parts of their bodies *Culture?*"

Again he pointed to one-woman panel. "Is that *Culture*—what those women gyrating to the ground in their undersized panties and showing that part of their bodies that only their husbands and gynecologists should see?"

The woman who answered Robinson could work for the FBI, CIA, and Scotland Yard on secondment away from her job as a sociologist at Medgar Evers College. She had no emotions on the podium. I had tried countless times to read her countenance but each time my subjective findings were spasmodic depending on how long I looked at her poker face.

That woman was Dr. Eli Balboza. She was nerdy cool without dark shades. She was nicely dressed, her head covered with a colorful Martiniquan head-wrap with her partly-curly, golden hair flowing out gently unto the nape of her neck. Her spice complexion glowed from the incandescence of the mantles above her. She answered Robinson with the calmness of the sound of water coming from a brook and flowing through rocks in the dense forest. She began, "*Culture* is what you do or create; it is everything in society that pertains to our family, our politics, our economics, our education, our religion—all these things fall within the ambit of culture, Mr. Robinson."

She looked at him.

"*Culture* is what holds a society together—your ideas, your ideologies, abstract and non-abstract; material and immaterial, including the gyrating to the ground by the women on Eastern Parkway is *Culture.*" She lowered her voice as low as the sound of sand at ebb tide."Be informed, sir, that *Culture* is universal, and its manifestations are different here in Brooklyn than what is in the Bronx even though we are all part of New York."

My sleeping gear was wet with perspiration because no matter how hot it is, I must cover with a blanket. But my sweating under the blanket didn't stop me from dreaming of the *Joseph Robinson-Eli Balboza Debate* on *Culture* in the Medgar Evers College Jackson Auditorium. I sat on the chair behind Robinson, and I should have forewarned him of Balboza's savvy from childhood.

Now my dreams were renewed, and I was reminded about what Balboza had told me what had happened to her when she was a little 8-year-old girl. She was the only child in her class of parents who didn't live from hand to mouth for survival in Trinidad. Her parents were not filthy rich, but their means were enough to cater for their one child to wear gold in cow pens, if they had any. When all the children walked to school barefooted on the hot asphalt, sometimes melting from the heat of the sun, the "Balboza girl," as the teachers had called her, had leather shoes, nice dresses that she changed every day, and a Panama hat to shade her from the tropical sun.

The children, especially the girls whose parents were dirt poor, were jealous of that Balboza girl. They called her "Miss Panama Hat." The haters provoked her to fight them knowing that she was puny in build. The haters' weapon for beating the Balboza girl was holding on to her hair which fell from her skull to her waist. Those evil, little girls pulled her hair, ran with her hair in their hands, pulled her to the ground, and laughed to their hearts' content.

Balboza learned how she should retaliate to the enemy from her mother who made it her duty to teach her that the first science for survival is to be prepared for all eventualities. Hence, Balboza had a plan to combat the haters. First, she got rid of her Panama hat and gave her mother a reason why she doesn't need it. "Mama, the wind is always blowing off my hat. Once

I ran to get it, and I was almost hit by a Mack truck."
Her mother loves her little girl and wanted nothing to
harm her, so her mother bought a beret.

"Mama, the gym teacher says *washikong* (ten-
nis shoes) is better for our daily netball practice. He
says when I jump in my leather shoes I can hurt the
child in front of me." Her loving mother acceded to
her request and bought her the *washikong*.

The day was December 6, Balboza's birthday.
The girls ganged up to beat puny Balboza on her birthday because they thought Balboza's long hair was always at their command to hold, fold, and pull. But
Balboza was playing the haters' game. As the haters
ran for her long hair, she ran ahead of them, jammed
her hair to the wall, and let her feet do the kicking
like Bruce Lee's. As each opponent tried to get her se-
cured hair, each got her full blast that came from her
knees and toes that were solidly padded. She kicked
the chief bully so hard that that bully cried aloud, and
the others scattered like flitted flies not wanting to feel
the force from the feet and knees of the little Balboza
girl on her birthday.

Had Robinson in his Debate on Culture known
of Balboza's savvy from girlhood, he would have listened and would have learned that Culture is like lo-

calized showers that fall on only one side of the street, sometimes. And he, sometimes, should listen, and learn from listening.

Between sleep and wake, I felt something cold on my face. I sleep as a dead man, and the coldness on my face didn't even stir me. I turned, and the coldness seemed to be part of my dream. Then the coldness was pressed firmly on my neck; it was released, pressed again, and then unmoved. I half-opened my sticky eye-lids, and my sticky eye-lids closed effortlessly. Then I was pushed.

"Get up! I hate you!"

Sill groggy with sleep, I caught the voice. "Whassup, brother?"

"You are not my fuckin brother. You are a traitor! You are fuckin my wife."

"Hector, why are you putting that gun in my face? I left the door opened for you." I knew I lied. I was too tired to close the door last night.

"You sent away my wife after you fucked her. You have to find her else I'll kill both of you."

"Hector, will you move that gun from my face, and let me get up, please."

"Get up and sit on the bed. Don't forget I have a fuckin gun."

"You have your gun so why curse."

"Where did you send my wife to hide from me?"

"I haven't seen you or your wife for over two years. I know nothing about that woman—your wife." My mind ran on a certain President when I said, "That woman."

"I'm tired of your lies. You said you didn't know who Gordon is."

"Hector, Gordon is a *Facebook* character that your wife Zelda invented."

"And you had told me that you didn't know who that cocksucker is."

"How could I know him? He's not my brother, Seth. I'm going to make breakfast. I'm making for two. Please, take that gun out of my face. Don't behave as if you have a novice's brain. Remember what Dr. Balboza told us when she discussed behavioral sociology with us. By the way, she's coming to see me today."

I sensed he was relaxing because his eyes no longer had that murderous look, and I stopped talking. Hector rested his gun down and walked away from it. I stayed away from the gun because I suspected he had another gun, and the gun he rested down may have no bullets. And probably he wanted me to draw with that gun to kill me in self-defense.

My thought could be wrong. But from our many years of friendship he made up tricks to get me napping or rushing for the wrong gift bag that Zelda brought for us. He outsmarted me every time when Zelda left two gift bags on the dining table and said, "Guys, anyone can choose first." I always picked up the gift I hated because of Hector's antics. That in mind, I told myself I will never rush to grab that gun lying on the counter. That's a trick.

Breakfast was on the table. Nothing fancy: whole wheat bread, Jamaican water cracker, Jamaican hard dough, butter, sausage with fried eggs, avocado, coffee, orange juice, milk, and brown sugar in a jar. Hector said whenever he eats Jamaican hard dough bread it reminds him of a Jamaican woman he had loved, but he had to let her go because she was always asking for money to send barrels of goods back to Jamaica. I know he had given her money to send five barrels one year.

"Let's eat, Hector. Put away your gun." He reluctantly put it in his coat pocket.

"How you got in?"

"Aren't you glad to see me, man?"

"Sure. Serve yourself."

Hector ate as if he saw food for the first time in months. When we were finished eating, I said, "I'll bet one hundred dollars to your five that the gun you put in your jacket pocket has no bullets."

He didn't take the bet, and I didn't repeat the bet. "I didn't put water on the table, Hector. Bring two glasses for us. I bought a new keyboard. Do you think you'll find time to teach me to play like you when you have spare time?"

"I have plenty time. I'm not working."

"Why?"

"I'm suffering from depression."

"How much time Homeland gave you?"

"Six months."

"Are you taking your meds?"

"No."

"Why?"

"Nothing is wrong with me."

I looked at my friend. "Are you still grieving for Betsy?"

"I never stopped grieving of her. The terrorists' bomb should have killed me instead."

I stopped my questioning.

"Where is Zelda, Stude Bakka?"

"Hector Hedgpine, the last time I'd seen her was when she was with you, and that's over two years ago. Why do you think I should know her whereabouts?"

"Because she confided in you. And I still believe you boned her when I was away on my stupid job."

"You want me to swear on the Bible that I never boned her? Don't forget Dr. Balboza told us a woman hides not what she wants you to know. And she stressed a woman is the family engineer; family is the most important institution of our socialization, and she believed you and Zelda were like children playing family-dolly house and hide and seek. She will be here any minute."

Hector smiled, and I knew that smile because it telegrammed he was lightening up and hate left his eyes. His eyes become gray when he is angry and ready to kill.

Once a man stepped on his toes on a bus, and the man refused to apologize. The next thing I knew his eyes became gray and the man was lying on the floor on his back from the blow from Hector's boots. He showed his ID to the bus driver to stop the bus, and said, "Some people think they own the world. For sure, that scum owns my boots."

I looked at him, and he changed the subject.

"Stude, what Balboza's into?"

"She is a Senior Research Fellow, Caribbean Research Center, Professor of Social and Behavioral Sciences at Medgar Evers College, and archivist and researcher in carnival traditions. I have attended her seminars, and her discussions on family dynamics will blow your mind. Nothing is too private to discuss in her seminars."

"Nothing?"

"Nothing. In one of her seminars she was discussing a rite of a boy to manhood. The theme of that discussion was about a thirty-year old woman who broke in a seventeen-year-old boy into loving sex. Most of the women in the seminar were saying, 'That thirty-year-old bitch should go to jail.'" I looked at Hector and asked, "You think that thirty-year-old woman should go to jail for teaching the seventeen-year-old boy how to enjoy sex?"

"If it is safe sex, that's all right with me. What did Dr. Balboza tell those women in the seminar?"

"She changed the subject to a completely new discussion. She asked the men, 'Who went to bed with one woman, put up your hands?' Not a single man put up his hand. Then she asked, 'How many men here had gone to bed with many women?' All the men raised their hands and roared like lions in heat, even those men who were sitting next to their wives and girlfriends.

"Dr. Balboza segued, purposely, and had a discussion on dreams and how whenever she dreams of snakes she interprets that dream as having an enemy in her family. All or nearly all the women raised their hands to talk of their dreams. One woman said whenever she dreams of blood, she bets on the numbers, and she always wins. Another said when she dreams of having sex with a stranger, she knows for sure her man is getting it outside.

"A man said he always dreams of having sex, and whenever his wife wakes up she tells him, 'Honey, someone raped me last night when I was sleeping, and he did it better than you.' The room with the seminarians became noisier than a Caribbean fish market on Holy Thursday when everybody is jostling to buy fish to end the Lenten season with a bang.

"Dr. Balboza segued back to her original discussion and asked, 'All the women who have had sex with many men raise your hands?' Only one woman raised her hand.

"Then the old sage said, 'I think it is time to

break now. See you next week, and our discussion will be on *Culture*. I want you to give me your true feelings, women, of Pharaohs in ancient Egypt who could marry their daughters but not their mothers. I would also discuss how 'Culture is universal but its manifestations are unique to where you live and the times in which you live."'

That was the first time in over two years Hector and I had such laughter. We were two laughing idiots, laughing as if laughing gas had been pumped into us. It wasn't the effect of laughing gas but the way Dr. Balboza measured those hypocrites with the white of her eyes—those women who said they only slept with their husbands. Then she said, "See you next week, ladies." Dr. Balboza spoke with her eyes. She was like Jesus telling the accusers of the harlot woman, "Ye who are without sin cast the first stone."

The phone rang, and Hector answered it laughing like a hyena. "Who are you?" The phone was on speaker.

"Dr. Joanna Elizabeth Haye."

"The call is for me, Hector." I took the phone. "Dr. Jo. are you in circulation?"

"Yes. And I bought three tickets: one for me, one for Vic, and one for you to see *PEEPING THROUGH*

THE KEYHOLE. The play is back at Princeton."

"What!" Hector shouted.

"Who made that noise?" Dr. Haye asked.

"That's my buddy. His name is Hector Hedg-pine."

"Stude, you called me in LA to find out about this play. You begged me to call Dr. Gammie to find out where the play is. I tracked her down for you to find out when the play is coming to Princeton; and now you are refusing to go.

"I thought you wanted to see that play with Zorro Zorro and May May, that Venezuelan woman, who was once an illegal alien and couldn't speak English, and she married a man because she was hungry.

"Stude, my hair stood up at the back of my neck all through the play; and I never could have imagined the ending of the play. I will be seeing that play for the second time. Vic doesn't want me to go back to watch me cry. I cried to see the emotional and physical abuse May May suffered at the hands of a man."

"Dr. Jo, give my ticket to your mother."

There was a pause in our conversation

"Dr. Jo, Hector and I saw that play from its inception."

"Stude, that couldn't be! That play just came

back from Australia with great reviews in the Australian presses. Stop lying and come to see the play with us. If you wish, I can buy two more tickets for Georgia and my father, and I will put all of you up at Nassau Inn as when you came to my Ph.D. Defense." She hung up, disgusted that I would not come to the play.

I became silent and looked at Hector. He became a chameleon changing colors; his eyes were glued to the speaker, and his eyes became gray. Neither of us noticed when Dr. Balboza came into the room. Neither did we know for how long Dr. Eli was there, and listening to the conversation on the speaker phone.

"Hi, Guys."

"Dr. Eli, how did you get in?" I asked.

"Stude, the door was not locked."

"Dr. Eli, this is Hector. Do you remember him?"

"Sure!"

"Hector, do you remember her?"

"Sure! Dr. Balboza, Stude and I call your name umpteen times as day. I'm so glad to meet you again."

"Guys, I would be happy to discuss the play with you."

"You saw it Dr. Eli? When?" I shouted

"My cousin, Arthur—I had introduced him to you at my last carnival discussion at the United Nations—lives in Princeton, New Jersey, and he invited me to see the play."

"What do you think of the play?" I asked

"May May, the lead actor, was very good. She is an expert in retailing love in the ratio of an elephant for herself and a rabbit for the men she loves; and she loves none. She loves sex in a cavalier way. She has a beautiful body; she has a beautiful Spanish-English accent; and she's a nymph. When sex becomes stale with the last man, she gets a new one. As a sociologist, I told my son who thinks he is Don Juan, that he could never fathom a woman if even she's chained to his back pocket." She looked at Hector and me. And Hector surprised us when he spoke.

"Dr. Balboza, nice meeting you again; and I am sure we'd never meet again."

"Hector, what do you mean by 'we'd never meet again?'"

He gripped her hand as if they were in combat. "Goodbye, Dr. Balboza. Stude, lock your door."

"When Dr. Eli and I speak our doors are never locked. Take care, my friend."

"You, too, my brother." He looked at me as if he had Jesus' cross to bear.

Dr. Balboza went outside and made sure Hector was out of sight. "Stude, Hector called you *my brother.* Why didn't you call him *my brother?*"

"He stopped me from calling him my brother."

"That's interesting. Tell me anything about Hector and why he stopped you from calling him brother. Tell me about his family life; his job; whether he likes music—sad songs, jumpy songs, Sinatra or Kanye West; his love life...anything."

"While Dr. Haye was speaking about the play, he was grieving."

"How do you know that?"

"His color was changing as a chameleon, and his eyes got gray. I know all his moods."

"I came in the room on time to hear Dr. Haye inviting you to see PEEPING THROUGH THE KEY-HOLE, and you bluntly refused to go. Yet you were like a crazy man calling her in Los Angeles and anywhere you can find her to know where the play is taking place. Now why are you refusing to go and see the play with her?"

I played dumb and changed the subject, but Dr. Balboza was not buying my dumbness.

"Stude, why you don't want to see the play? You and I know the play speaks of Zelda's guile. She fucked up your head too, and you are afraid she'd be laughing at you and Hector, the two fools, in the audience."

I kept silent.

She shouted, and shouting is not her habit. She always treats me with utter respect. "Stude Bakka, are you holding secret for that vanilla man?"

"What do you want to know?"

"Everything about him and his parents."

"I don't know them. He told me about them; and I told him about mine."

"I am not interested in your parents. What he told you about his parents?"

"His mother had a man with his father, and his father killed her."

"How did his father find out?"

"By searching and finding her savings account, he calculated that her salary and his, minus expenses, could not make up the large sum in her savings account. He said he was sure the money was coming from her lover, and he knew her lover. He told that to the judge who sentenced him to life without parole."

"Money could be coming from her own hidden fortune," Dr. Eli said

"Hector's father knew everything about his mother from the day they were married and before; and he knew she had no hidden fortune."

"I think there is more to that story that you are unwilling to tell. What about his music?"

"He's a keyboardist. He loves to play sad songs. Before you came he was playing his composition *Betsy, Where are You Now?* And it was like redeeming a pledge. Dr. Eli , what is the word when one is redeeming a pledge?"

"Degage."

"That's it! It was as if he were afraid to touch the white notes on the keyboard. When he touched C, it was as if that note was dirty."

"Who is Betsy?"

"That was his dog."

"Where is Betsy? Is she in the pound for biting someone?"

"She is dead."

"Old age?"

"A bomb killed her. Hector is sick in his heart because Betsy gave her life for him. He says he is responsible for Betsy's death."

"How?"

"By Betsy stepping on a terrorist's bomb. This

country has more home-grown terrorists than we are willing to admit. Hector works for Homeland Security, and he was on a certain beat. Betsy walked ahead of him, and was pulling Hector one way. It seemed Hector had Zelda's worries on his mind and did not obey Betsy's sniffing senses. He pulled Betsy the wrong way, and before Betsy could jump as she is trained to do, the bomb exploded.

"Betsy died, but Hector was seriously injured. He blames himself day after day for Betsy's death. Up to this day, Hector is a wrecked soul; he has no patience; and his reasoning is bare. He came early this morning and awoke me with his gun on my neck."

"Why?"

"He said I'm screwing his wife. I don't think they are married, but they behave as if they are."

"Like May May and Zorro Zorro in the play."

I became mute. And I could feel her pupils searching mine. She addressed me formally.

"Mr. Bakka, I know nothing about séance, and you don't want to see that play because you and Hector are the voices in that play. Both of you are round characters played by someone else in that play. Why don't you ask me how do I know that?"

I refused to ask her. I know for sure that Dr. Eli

Balboza is no fool. I had been in many of her seminars on family dynamics, in social gatherings with her, and I watched the different ways she studied her audience. I can tell when she looks up at a person, and then down with an empty smile. Both looks are in juxtaposition of each other, and like a psychiatrist on the stool, and we, her patients, sitting on the sofa, she juts down notes. And I am not excluding myself. I know when she's studying me.

My mind went wondering on the past with Hector. But Dr. Balboza brought me back to the present with her crisp, short sentences.

"What is Zelda's maiden name? How long have they been in love? Where they met? What she does for a living? How good is her English now? What is her vocation and avocation? What she does in her spare time? Why did Hector suspect that you are fucking her?"

I answered all her questions.

"Stude, you ever thought of googling Zelda?"

"No."

"A family friend in the sacred sanctum of government once told me he owes me one for what I've done for him when he was a bad boy. I'll call him now to repay me today. Give me another coffee, black."

I brought the coffee. She took out her cell phone, and put the person on speaker who answered, "XL." Dr. Eli spoke in Trini gibberish and Pidgin English combined. XL answered with the same idioms, and hung up. I knew what both parties were saying because all children my age spoke gibberish in Fyzabad, and especially Pidgin English when we mocked the Chinese immigrants who were shopkeepers.

"Dr. Eli , do you remember the Pidgin English joke with the two China men in court?"

"Sure. But I'm not in the mood for jokes now. Where do you think Hector is now?"

"I don't know."

"How long he is separated from Zelda?"

"I don't know. He doesn't know that they are not officially married."

"Were you humping Zelda?"

"I swear."

"I don't want you to swear. Answer yes or no."

"No."

"I'm expecting a call about Zelda."

"From whom?"

"Your business is just to listen, and don't ask questions." She looked at me as when she looks at a student who is always interrupting her, who thinks he is smarter than she, but she knows he is shallow as the back of a fiction book cover.

Dr. Eli's cell rang. "Shoot, XL."

"Party in question is Venezuelan Zelda Peña. Parents were close friends of one the most feared Dictators who taught her all there is to know about guns. Port of exit is Caracas. Port of entry is JFK. Customs in Caracas seized all her luggage and returned them to her parents. Thousands of US money was stored in her luggage.

"She married David Ide, a drug trafficker and gambler who served time. He has many aliases. Only one recorded marriage is shown.

"Interpol reports she's very smart but no threat to this country. She helped poor people in the slums in Caracas. She speaks many languages, but beside her native tongue, Spanish, she is proficient in Portuguese, French, and English.

"She writes stories in English for a children's magazine in Caracas. I can get the name of the magazine editor if you need it in a hurry. Literature is her hobby, and from childhood she had a knack to bring people together to create propos."

"What's propos, XL?"

"Propaganda. Her guile is unfathomable. I

got to go. Is your hair still very long, and do you still hide it when you are fighting? You didn't let me marry your daughter, but you are still my mother-in-law by proxy. One more thing, she studied in La Sorbonne." He hung up.

Dr. Eli looked at me, and her eyes said, "That woman fucked you up, fool. She's proficient in the English language... In Caracas, she writes for a children's magazine in English."

She picked up her car keys, kissed me on my forehead the way my mother kissed me when she had the strap hidden behind her back in her left hand to get a good grip of me with her right hand before she flogged me for eating my stepfather's dinner after I ate mine.

`She commanded me: "Lock your door, Stude. Hector is not coming back. You have to find him before he kills Zelda. He feels you fucked his wife, but you are not his problem. But Zelda is, for her promiscuity with Zorro Zorro."

I kept mumbling, "Zee's proficient in English... Zee's proficient in English...Zee's proficient in English. "

8

I t took me long to sleep. I kept repeating, "Zee's proficient in the English language." I was tempted to take an *Ambien* sleeping pill but I changed my mind knowing what it did to my brain: I used to go sleep walking, go and cook, paint, and do other crazy things at nights.

Suddenly, I remembered Dr. Haye had told me the play would be showing tomorrow at Princeton University. I had no intention of seeing that play. I felt like getting on a plane and go to South Africa to see my granddaughter, Soley. Then, I again went back to the chorus, "Zee's proficient in the English language."

Then I burst out in a new chorus. "No! No! Zee is like *Ambien*. She fucked up Hector's brain. I must find him before he kills her. He was listening to what Dr. Haye had said about the play."

I remember Hector telling me, "Zelda thinks she's so fucking smart. My mother thought she was smarter than my father too."

Preparation anxiety the next morning cramped my lucidity. I could not find my clothes. Since my last helper left after I buried my wife, whenever I washed I put my clothes here, there, and everywhere. There was no system of domestication in my house because I was never in a hurry to find anything after my wife died. With fits and starts, I got dressed. I looked in the mirror, and I saw a clown.

Once my granddaughter, A'dhayna, asked her aunt, "Why does grandpa wear the same clothes every time and his eyebrows move sometimes?"

I realized that I was dressed as a clown when I boarded the train to Princeton. All the mirrors at Penn Station did not lie about my appearance. It was 6 p.m. when I bought my round trip from Penn Station to Princeton Junction. I counted the stops to Princeton Junction on the monitor. I knew I would not reach Princeton for the first Act, and that was okay. I knew what that Act would be: Hector and I wrote all the Acts in our heads; we are just not on stage.

As the trains passed towns after towns, I felt a chill in my body, and I shouted the names of the stations: Secaucus Junction, Newark Penn Station, Newark International Airport. It was a sad chill as when my wife had died in bed next to me, and I was still hugging her. I did not realize my wife had died until the helper came in to clean her. I dare not say what I was really thinking on my way to find Hector. So I let my mind go back to the good times Hector, Zelda, and I had.

We were a trio-in-friendship-and-family love. We teased each other; we put our forks in each other's dish and tasted each-other's food. Hector and I always discussed how such a play will end. I dare not say, "Yes, Hector," but I wished the play ends as he acted it out as an imaginary play.

But I knew my wish was a wasted wish when he sang and played on the keyboard, *There Will Never Be Another Like You*. He did not play it with a jazzy beat as he usually does when both of us changed places on the keyboard, and we improvised. This time he played it as a death march as if he were accompanying a trumpeter playing *Taps for a departed soldier at Arlington Cemetery*.

Hector's idea was at each play Zelda would be wearing a diaphanous gown. She would drop a piece of her garment at each play; and on her last play, the tenth, she would drop her gown and be naked. I pretended I was not listening to what would be happening on the final day of *PEEPING THROUGH THE*

KEYHOLE, SHE LEARNED ABOUT LIFE, AND LOVE, AND ABOUT SEX.

I was aware that he had suspected that I'd crossed the boundary he had set for me with his wife. I had never crossed that boundary, physically, with his wife; but I'd pay a king's ransom to be an artist to paint her on canvas.

Her booty, fitted with spanx, moves without invitation; her grapefruit breasts, covered minimally, reminded me of Miss Root's breasts. She was the woman who taught me sex at seventeen. All I was thinking of was getting in the space between Zelda's legs. Nevertheless, I never got into that space. I honored my friendship with Hector, a white man, born in Austin, Texas. He was the only white man I came close to. We were like blood brothers.

I was born and bred in Fyzabad and from childhood I never had a white friend nor was even close to one that I can touch to see if my blackness would rub off on his whiteness. My mother was a washerwoman who worked for a white family. The main building and servants' quarters were on a hill, and my mother could see when her boss's jitney was approaching the hill top.

Her boss, Mr. Mowl, was an oil driller, and an

expatriate from England. My mother would push me inside to hide because neither Mr. nor Mrs. Mowl knew I was in the servants' quarters; and when they had given my mother permission to bring me to work with her, their stern warning was, "Mary, do not let Stude go outside to play with the other children." My mother thought I did not know why she said that. So she lied to me. Why did parents of my mother's ilk think their black children were dumb to the prejudices their parents suffered from those British expatriates in the oilfields?

My only thought was on my dear friend, Hector, whom I love. And he loves me unconditionally. He gave me money when I lost my job. We chatted about life, about America, about the Caribbean, about Texas that wants to go it alone, and about the prejudices in our democracy. We disagreed; but we agreed to disagree.

Once he told me, "Stude Bakka, I'm not a Christian; neither am I a stupid man like you who are always looking for rainbows to paint."

"Hector Hedgpine, if I were a Christian, I would have fucked your wife rather than dreaming of fucking her."

"Let's drink to that, you fuckin atheist." We

laughed endlessly.

I was sure he was on his way to Princeton to see *PEEPING THROUGH THE KEYHOLE.* I was also sure he'd be in dark clothing and disguised not to be easily identified. But even if he were a black cat in a black room I'd discern him. He never sits with his back to a door. No matter how the chairs are arranged his back is on an angle. And if he's annoyed or agitated his vanilla color glows.

Another of his tactics is to get a seat near a child or a woman. Once I asked him why? His answer was, "That's a Homeland secret."

Sometimes he went as a transgender to work. When Dr. Balboza told me to close my door because Hector will not be coming back, that was not an original thought. I, too, thought of that. My phone was on speaker, so when he stepped out of my house I knew he had heard what Dr. Haye had told me when she called to invite me to the last showing of the play at Princeton Lewis Thomas 003 Hall. His color changed. And whenever his color changed to vanilla it was always a bad omen that I had observed over the years that we have been close friends.

Then I remember he emptied the revolver's chamber but he left two bullets in it. "Oh my god!

Don't let it be. Why isn't this fucking train moving? I want to reach in time for Act 2, no later!"

The man behind me said, "I paid to be in this noiseless car. Why don't you go in the other car and spew your vulgarity?"

"Fuck you, red negra. Why not take your hand and lead me to the other car as if I'm a blind man?" He didn't have to talk to me a second time when I saw the ticket examiner walking into the car. I ran out that car like a deer with wet feet escaping from a hungry hunter. But my speed did nothing to the stationary train. The train engineer was waiting on the signal to move at Metuchen.

My mind was foreseeing things. "Don't do it, Hector." I put my both palms over my sweaty face and rubbed off one of my penciled eyebrows. Now I looked as a clown without lipstick and only one eyebrow because I was sweating cold and wiping off the sweat and penciled make-up on one side of my face. Then I shouted the name of the approaching stop: Edison. The train stayed a short time at New Brunswick and Jersey Avenue.

At last I reached Princeton Junction. I jumped to the platform, and ran for a taxi. I pushed away the woman in front of me.

"That woman was ahead of you, sir," the cabbie said.

"Let him go. What do you expect from...." I looked at her, and she didn't complete her sentence.

"Madam, sorry; I'm in a hurry. Cabbie, that nice lady said it's okay." I jumped in his car. "Take me to Princeton University. Do you know in which building that popular play, *PEEPING THROUGH THE KEYHOLE,* is showing tonight?"

"Earlier today I took a man from Brooklyn there. He was telling me to drive faster. You are from Brooklyn too?"

"Yes."

"You Brooklyn people have that attitude chip on your shoulders. You talk down to taxi drivers."

"Sorry, man. I'm in a hurry."

"You want me to fly over the vehicles in front of me, Mr. Brooklyn."

"I'm sorry, man. I just had a fight with my girlfriend who has another man, and I'm mad. Could you, please, describe the man you brought earlier today and dropped at Princeton University?"

"Sort of vanilla color. He was talking to himself saying crazy things about suicide and all that shit. I was glad when that fool got out of the car, but he gave me a big tip as if money meant nothing to him."

My breath stopped. I was gasping for air when I heard the cabbie's description of the vanilla man and his intention.

"What's wrong with you, Mr. Brooklyn?"

I had both palms in my face. In two days I heard the description of *that* man as vanilla. Could it be the same man?

I opened both windows to get New Jersey's garden-state air while breathing through my mouth. "What is blocking the fucking traffic today...on the train...on the road." I looked at the clock on the cabbie's dashboard and shook my head. "The second Act is almost over." In another two minutes I was there.

In the Lewis Thomas 003 Hall, the very hall I went to hear Joanna Elizabeth Haye's Defense for her Ph.D., a man pretending to be an old man with a cane, was hiding his face.

He sat next to a little girl with pigtails, and he softly asked, "Do you like dogs? What's your name?" I read their lips. I'm very good at lip reading. Hector taught me. He had told me that was the only Homeland Security training he'll teach me.

"I like dogs, and my name is Nancy. And what is your name? You look like my grandpa."

The pretender did not answer her question, but said, "I like dogs a lot." The pretender remained quiet, but he was fidgety as if a bug was walking in his crotch, and nipping him in the hairy place every now and then.

The pretender looked at the program in his hand, then at his wrist watch to gauge when the final Act will begin. "My dog's name is Betsy. What's your dog's name?"

"I just call her puppy, puppy. I like your dog's name."

"Well, take that name for your new dog if you like it. I have a picture of Betsy, and I will give it to you when the play is over. I will like to meet your parents to tell them how to take care of your new Betsy because I will be giving it to you."

"I will tell my father Betsy is my new name for my dog."

The pretender told the little girl, "Hold this. Betsy's picture is in this envelope. Oh! Oh! I'm having a pain. Go and call somebody in charge to come and help me." The pretender groaned softly.

"My father is in charge. I will run and call him."

"Wait! Wait! I will tell you when to run and call him."

"Okay. Can I look at Betsy's picture now?"

"Not yet."

9

"This is Act 10, the last Act, and the last day for this play. The promoter of this great play has told no one when this play will be seen again," the announcer with a paunch and an executive haircut said.

May May Maryland and Zorro Zorro woke up. Zorro Zorro was lying in the back of the bed, and his role ended when he kissed May May passionately.

That's when I got a better view of the play and saw where the pretender, a man with his cane, was seated as a decoy. I knew it was Hector. He was writing something on colored paper; and then he put the paper he was writing on in an envelope. The room was dark, and only the stage was lit.

I tried to barge my way to get to Hector. I remembered the layout of Lewis Thomas 003 Hall because I was there three months ago for Dr. Joanna Elizabeth Haye Defense for her Ph.D. in molecular biology. I was all over that hall, and I shot three rolls of film of people with my camera. But today I did not walk with my camera. I walk with both hands to get close to Hector and grab him firmly because I know what he has in mind.

I pushed the man who was blocking my view to the stage very hard. He was an undercover cop. The undercover cop next to him gripped me firmly. Then both of them held my both arms as if I were a piece of luggage to be thrown into the hole with other cargo on Delta Airlines.

I pleaded, "Officer, I'm sorry for pushing you. Please, let me go to help my sick friend."

"You are the sick one. He's probably looking for you, sicko."

I screamed, "Hector, Hector, don't do it! Zee, Zee, don't drop your gown! Hector has two bullets in his revolver; one for you, and one for him."

As the policemen were dragging me, I screamed as loud as a fire engine, "Zee, don't take the final bow. Run for your life."

Both cops lifted me out bodily and dropped me outside. One said, "I'm sure he doesn't have a green card. I feel to lock him up."

The other cop said, "Give him a break. If he comes back inside we'll lock him up."

I sat on the edge of the concrete step. I put both index fingers in my ears and prayed. "Don't let it happen, Lord."

My life went back in time, and I remembered I had taken off speaker tone when Dr. Haye related the last scene: "May May will come to the edge of the stage, sing *Everybody's Somebody's Fool,* and bow to her audience. She will make a short, but tearful speech tracing her life from the age of five to the last day of the play."

Hector knew why I took the phone off speaker: When he had read the sex text sent to him, by mistake, instead of to Gordon, he had threatened her. She used her guile and her body to tell him, "Honey, you and I could act that part." She had hugged him and placed his head in her bosom. She had expected him to nibble on her nipples, his patented foreplay, but he didn't.

She continued with her guile. "Honey, think of you and me in that play, and in the last scene I'll drop the last piece of my garment. We will have ten shows, and in every show I will drop one piece of clothes; and in the very last show I will drop my last piece of clothes. The world will see the beautiful physique that God has given me for you only. Our audience will cheer and cheer. The encores will be constant."

"You'll really do that, Zelda." He moved away from her.

"It's just my imagination, honey."

"I hope it is just your imagination, Zelda, or else!"

"Hector, all my life my eyes were on the ball; and that ball is America. I ran away from riches to be burlesqued in America. I thank you for what you have done for me. Your decision is not and will never be mine. I am living in my truth. I am not nervous because you are standing next to me and frightening me with your evil eyes. I am prepared to have Betsy's fate; and you can be the terrorist."

He did not reply. I knew when he was silent he was most dangerous, and never backs away from his evil intentions. He was still wearing the black mourning band on his left arm.

That was the last time they lived under the same roof. Zelda dropped the document on the floor that should have been sent to the City Registrar to register their marriage in the eyes of the law. Hector picked it up, his eyes icy, "So we are not married, bitch!...You are worse than the terrorist who killed Betsy."

He took his 8-foot ladder, opened it on the

flooring, climbed on it, stretched his hand, and ripped off something from the ceiling. It was a tape recording of her forcing me to have sex with her. I always suspected his apartment was wired.

She was not a bit phased by him knowing she was forcing me to make love to her.

I've studied that Venezuelan woman. She's "into manners." She is always very polite. She was born into high society; but she was also born "into diplomacy, living on the edge as her mother, and staying alive with guile in all its excesses."

She was schooled by one of Venezuela's most vicious Dictators. She had confided in me after her first husband had kicked her that she will never abide by the dictates of any man. Not even if he is Lucifer.

"What do you mean, Zee?" I'd asked.

"Stude Bakka, I will rather die looking into my assassin's barrel of his gun than succumb to him. It will be the last Act in my once sad but now happy moment in the United States of America. There will be peace in my heart when I'm taken back to Caracas to be put in our family's tomb to be buried next to my mother who gave up her life and her happiness for me to go abroad."

"When she died?" I had asked her and tried

to relive that moment to remember how her mother died.

I couldn't think of when her mother died because the decibel sounds of two bullets hurt my ear drums and foiled my thinking as I lay on the concrete.

The sounds confirmed murder of two or by two: Hector found his target. His bullet pierced the middle of Zelda's forehead.

Zelda found her target, too. She had the revolver that she had stolen from David Ide. She was as good a marksman as Hector or better. Her bullet came through the pocket in her black gown.

She fell from the stage into Hector's arm. Both assassins opened their eyes for the last time, looked at each other as lovers do, hugged, and fell on the floor. They were dead.

Zelda didn't shed her gown, and it wasn't diaphanous, purposely. It was black cotton. Her revolver was hidden in the inside pocket, and it could not be seen. That is the part in Zelda's play that was never revealed in advance. It was in nobody's flyer or in Hector's conceived plan. His Homeland Security smarts couldn't trump her I.Q.

Once she had told Hector when he had threatened her, "I know you fear me more than you love me."

He replied with a cold grin as Richard Wind-
mark's, "Zelda, you are no Delilah."

She smiled, "Hector, you are no Samson."

I was shocked by Zelda's smarts when I read
the full police report: "Zelda Hedgpine was ambidex-
trous. She moved off the bed with her left hand in her
pocket and studied the pretender with the broad hat
and cane after a cursory glance at her audience. She
bowed and waved to the vast audience with her right
hand as she came to the edge of the stage.

"Hector fired first, and so did she with the distance of a split-atom second after him with her left
hand that was always on the trigger of her revolver.

"He was a Homeland Security marksman. She
had studied ballistics with the Dictator three times
a week; and Russian roulette was her game. She pretended to be a *Facebook* lover, but strategy and murder was her love.

"After he shot her, he smiled. He raised his gun
slowly to his head to commit suicide, but she would
not let him have that victory to show his love for her.
That victory had to be hers; and it was hers: She shot
the gun out of his hand, and her smile of death was
victorious. She killed him with the last bullet in her

revolver."

I read the police report countless times.

I will always remember Zelda's words: "Stude Bakka, I am not like Jesus. I will not turn the other cheek." And she lived by her words.

Like Martin Greenfield, President Barack Obama's tailor who speaks of the Holocaust with sadness, I will recycle the advice that his father gave him and apply that advice to myself when thinking of my deceased friends, Hector and Zelda Hedgpine: "I will honor your life by living and thinking of the good times we have had, not by crying."

It was written in *Princeton News* that the crowd cheered noisily for several minutes: "PEEPING, PEEPING, PEEPING." Then three more words: "ENCORE! ENCORE! ENCORE!" The yellow curtain was drawn for the cast to come out, bow, and acknowledge the thunderous applause. Only Zorro Zorro came forth, and he bowed graciously.

———————

The little girl ran to her father and showed him the envelope that the unknown man gave her. "Open it, Nancy. It's yours."

She did. "It is Betsy's picture, daddy." She gave her father the envelope.

"There's something else in the envelope, Nancy."

"You open it, daddy."

He did. "It is a letter to you, Nancy."

"Read it, daddy."

He gasped. "It is a check for ten thousand dollars drawn to Cash. In memo line is BUY A NEW BETSY, AND TAKE CARE OF HER."

10

D r. Balboza got hold of me after three weeks because I was not answering phone calls.

"Dr. Eli, everything is in the Police hands. I just notice Hector left his coat in my clothes closet."

"Why not search it?"

"Hold on. I see a letter telling me where to bury him, and a check to cover my expenses."

"So he knew he was going to die."

She sensed I was choking up, and she waited till I felt better. I opened a book of Hector's poems, and I read few lines of *LIFE* to console my spirit: Life puckers up and down/ Its air is hot at times and stifling/ Cold at times and pains my aching bones/ But we need air to breathe/ The world is an imperfect globe/ But I love its imperfection all the way/ To my grave."

"Dr. Eli , do you like Hector's poem?"

"I do; but I have the feeling that Hector's life puckered down to the way he wanted to die. How their lives ended was a project of their high-mindedness and senseless pride. On paper they shared the same address, but they kept their unhappiness and evil intentions for each other hidden in their bosoms .

"That's why I hate when marriage counselors tell couples nonsense as an advice to 'hold on a little longer and your marriage will work.'

"Could you imagine a spouse and his transgender partner went to a marriage counselor for advice, and the marriage counselor told them to go to Lexington Plastic Surgeons for help knowing fully well that the couple's marriage wouldn't work because their complaint was: We never had sex before our marriage because it is a sin in the eyes of God to have sex before marriage. Whose fault is that? What could the plastic surgeons do?

"Before people thrust into marriage they should unwrap themselves for each other's benefit, and that is what Hector and Zelda failed to do during their courtship.

"She should have told him that she is a constant nymphomaniac, a chip off her mother's sexual block; she likes to be serviced and re-serviced erotically at any given time with lenses, filter, and lights focused on her.

"He should have told her his deep jealousy

would end in murder because he has no room in his heart for a woman who needs high maintenance in sex and must have many men between her legs. And worse still, he should have told her when Betsy died, life had no meaning.

"They should have had open discussions of what they can and cannot abide by; and their lives would not have ended in a tragedy but with an elixir of love for each other and a life of happiness.

"One of life's great imponderables is the way love should be measured and shared. Zelda and Hector treated sex as an event that one cannot pinpoint on a calendar of their hybrid living. Neither one knew what the other's circled date represents on the calendar. It could have been the date one would bounce out the other from this earth. Both straddled at the fence because neither knew how to express and share their love. They should know one can't put royalty on ignorance, on stupidity, and on hunger."

"Dr. Eli Balboza, I will remember your advice; and if I'm going to get married again, my future wife and I would come to you to unwrap us should we forget to unwrap ourselves. Is that a deal?"

"I'll be happy to do that for the future Mr. and Mrs. Stude Bakka."

I went to bed thinking of Dr. Balboza's wisdom and the knowledge of what life presents to mortals on this imperfect globe. I waited for daylight to hear her comforting voice. But all through the night I thought of the line in Hector's poem that reads, "Life puckers up and down." It reminds me of the secret he told me; and I vowed to him that I will never repeat it to anyone. But I will write it on his headstone. He had told me he'd write on my headstone, "The boy from Fyzabad has class."

The phone rang, and I rushed to answer it because I knew who would call me at that time. "Mr. Senior Citizen, I'm bringing breakfast for two."

"Thank you, Professor Balboza. The door will be wide opened. I hope you don't mind me playing over and over Michael Bublé singing *You and I* composed by Stevie Wonder."

"Is that your posthumous love song to your Zee?"

"That's not nice, Professor Balboza." We laughed. "Is it okay, if I play *You and I* when you come?"

"Mr. Senior Citizen, I only enforce rules in my class at Medgar Evers College."

"Then you can come, Professor."

"I hope you will let me read the draft of your new book, *Hector and Betsy*."

"And if I didn't?"

"No Wendy's breakfast for you, Grandpa."

"You always drive home the point that I am ten years older than you."

"More than ten years, Mr. Stude Bakka."

It was the first time in many months joyous laughter came from both of us.

"Dr. Eli, I'm always thinking of Hector who taught me 'The world is an imperfect globe,' and I knew what he meant by that metaphor. By the way, Professor Balboza, why is Lucy so selfish? She never let Charlie Brown kick the football."

"You are the author. Do the research for Sociology 101 next semester."

Our laughter echoed from dust to darkness, and morning met us speaking Pidgin English imitating the immigrant Chinese shopkeepers in Trinidad and Tobago during the ration of staple food during the World War II years, and laughing at each other's silly jokes.

Professor Eli Balboza interpreted Pidgin English in a sociological context and told me how the orient came about speaking English in the vernacular.

I was not listening. I was thinking and wishing that I'd *known* Zelda Hedgpine as in the biblical text.

The old sage read my mind. "Stude Bakka, friendship without sexual strings attached, is a beautiful thing."

Zelda Hedgpine's body was taken back to Caracas to be buried in the family's tomb next to her mother.

I wrote what Hector told me to write on his epitaph in Cypress Hill, Brooklyn, and I put flowers on his headstone on his birthday.

Whenever Hector comically reminded me what to write on his headstone during the jovial hours in their house, he'd go on the keyboard and imitate pianist Eldar D'jangirov's style of playing *What'll I Do*. He'd call Zelda. "Honey, I'm playing this for you." She'd kiss him. He'd slide on the long stool down to the base notes, and they'd play a duet. For my encore, they played *If I Should Lose You*, and I couldn't tell whose solo was better.

I couldn't call for an encore because their tears flooded each other's shoulder. I often wondered why.

During those times I could never have foreseen the way their lives would end.

And to know a woman of Zelda Hedgpine's

talents suffered the same fate as other nondescript abused women in America, and in my little oil town, Fyzabad, reminds me of Thomas Gray's *Elegy Written in a Country Church Yard*, in part: The dark unfathom'd caves of ocean bear:/ Full many a flow'r is born to blush unseen/ And waste its sweetness on the desert's air.

I should have recited that poem to Hector and Zelda to prevent them from hiding their sweetness for each other in Brooklyn's ethnic air where progressive Mayor Bill de Blasio resides.

Dr. Balboza invited me to meet her family in Long Island. I had a lovely time but not without her teasing. "Stude, one of my students at Medgar Evers College is teaching me educated *Ebonics*. Let me try out one on you."

"Shoot."

"Boy, you *was took* by that Venezuelan woman."

"And I enjoyed her *tooking*."

Our blast of laughter had Dr. Balboza's husband scampering downstairs to inquire what was that ruckus going on.

"Nothing," we said.

www.ingramcontent.com/pod-product-compliance
Lightning Source LLC
Chambersburg PA
CBHW070703280626

47159CB00022B/1795